Chal...

SOMEONE ...

I looked idly past Danny and then my jaw dropped in surprise. There was a stranger in the class. In the chair next to Danny was sitting a boy I'd never seen before in my life. Someone new. And what a someone! The stranger had wavy black hair and the sultriest pair of dark eyes I've ever seen in my life; they were staring at Olivia Strickland in a puzzled way, as though he had no idea what on earth she was talking about. He should join the club, I thought glumly. No one knows what Olivia is talking about most of the time. She has more brains than the rest of us put together.

I gave Danny a nudge. 'Who's that next to you?' I hissed. 'And what's his phone number?'

Chalfont College 1

Someone is Watching

LANCE SALWAY

Beaver Books

A Beaver Book

Published by Arrow Books Limited
62-65 Chandos Place, London WC2N 4NW

An imprint of Century Hutchinson Ltd

London Melbourne Sydney Auckland
Johannesburg and agencies throughout the world

First published by Piccadilly Press in 1987

Beaver edition 1989

Made and printed in Great Britain
by Anchor Press Ltd
Tiptree, Essex

ISBN 0 09 957300 8

CHAPTER ONE

I'll never forget the day it all started, the day I met Anton.
It was a Monday. I know it was a Monday because the day
began badly as Mondays often do, that Monday most of
all.

For a start, my alarm didn't go off, and I woke up half
an hour late and had to fling on yesterday's jeans and
forget about breakfast. Then my little brother, Theo,
threw up his muesli all over the kitchen floor and someone
– yes, me, you've guessed it – had to clean it up and clean
him up because Flanagan was in the shower. All this made
me even later, and I was in such a hurry to leave the flat
that I didn't notice until it was too late that it was pouring
with rain and I didn't have a coat or an umbrella with me.
And, as if that wasn't bad enough, I was halfway down the
road before I remembered that I'd left my *Macbeth* essay
half-finished on the desk in my bedroom. By the time I'd
rushed back upstairs for an umbrella and the essay, and
then rushed back down again into the rain, I was in a
blazing temper and in no mood for idle chatter with
Tammy-Ann Ziegler, who was standing at the bus stop
when I arrived there, wet, breathless and bad-tempered.

Tammy-Ann Ziegler isn't the best person to meet when
you're feeling wet, breathless and bad-tempered. She
never seems to be any of those things; she's always com-

1

posed, elegant and smiling, which is probably why I can't stand her. There's something about that long honey-blonde hair and year-round tan that never fails to get up my nose. It's jealousy, I suppose. Tammy-Ann always looks as though she's stepped straight out of a perfume commercial. She even looks good in the rain, and that made my Monday even worse.

'Hi, Mel,' she said when she saw me. 'What a day!'

'Yeah,' I muttered.

I'm no good at conversation before eleven in the morning but that didn't matter to Tammy-Ann. She chattered happily on about some Woody Allen movie she'd seen the night before with her latest boyfriend, and I just said, 'Really?' or 'Lucky you!' or 'Wow!' whenever she paused for breath. Tammy-Ann Ziegler likes the sound of her own voice, which is just as well because no one else does. The reason why she has a constantly changing string of boyfriends is that none of them can stand the sound of her voice for longer than a week at the most. Tammy-Ann may be beautiful but she sounds like a high-speed drill.

Tammy-Ann's shrill monologue about the new man in her life reminded me that I hadn't checked that morning to see if there was a letter from Jordan. Some hopes. What was it he'd told me when we said goodbye at Christmas? 'I'll write every week, I promise.'

'Every *day*,' I'd insisted. 'Every single day without fail.'

Jordan had given a loud groan. 'Give me a break, Mel. You know how I hate writing letters.'

'But you'll be writing to *me*,' I'd reminded him. 'Won't that make a difference?'

He put his arm around me and grinned. 'Sure it will,' he

2

said, and then kissed me gently on the forehead. 'It'll make all the difference in the world.'

The lying toad. The creep. Jordan had written three letters in January and another in February. It was now April and I hadn't heard from him at all since then. I'd written to *him*, of course. Every day to start with, and then once a week. I'd phoned him a couple of times, too, but it's a long way from London to Concord, New Hampshire, and my mother put a stop to the the calls when the phone bill came. Needless to say, Jordan hadn't phoned me at all. But what did phone calls matter? There'd be a letter from him tomorrow. Or the next day, maybe.

I looked at Tammy-Ann, who was still whining on about Shane or Wayne or whatever his name was. Drain, most probably. So what if boys didn't flock round me, at least I didn't have a voice like a rusty hinge. There was hope for me yet. But there seemed no hope of ever seeing a 74 bus. I usually walk to Chalfont, as it's not all that far from our building, but I didn't want to risk it in the rain. But, when ten minutes had passed with no sign of a bus, it looked as though I would have to.

'Look, I'm going to walk,' I said to Tammy-Ann. 'We'll never get there at this rate.'

'You're right,' she squawked, and together we set off along Prince Albert Road.

The rain began to ease as we walked and by the time we reached Chalfont it had stopped altogether. We turned in at the school gates and headed up the long tree-lined drive.

Chalfont School is tucked away at the end of this drive, well behind the houses and flats and chestnut trees that edge the quiet north London street. If it wasn't for the elegant stone pillars flanking the entrance and the discreet sign beside them that reads 'The Chalfont School', no one would ever guess that there is a school there at all. But, at the end of the drive, there are a couple of spacious playing fields and then the main building, which is Victorian with lots of turrets and stained-glass windows and was once a mansion called Chalfont Grange. The classrooms behind it were added much later, and are built mainly of glass, which makes them hot in summer and freezing cold in winter. None of this can be seen from the street, though, which is why visitors are always taken by surprise when they come to the school for the first time.

The rest of the class were already in their places by the time Tammy-Ann and I arrived, bedraggled and out-of-breath. At least, *I* was bedraggled and out-of-breath but Tammy-Ann, of course, looked as though she'd just emerged from a beauty parlour.

The class was English Literature with Jim Curtis; I suddenly remembered my unfinished essay and hoped that he wouldn't pick on me, today of all days. I shot him a damp, bright smile and said, 'Sorry we're late. We waited ages for a bus . . .'

He looked at me gravely and said, 'That's okay, Melanie. Sit down.'

I hate being called Melanie and he knows it. My mother named me after that wimpish Melanie in *Gone with the Wind* and I don't think I'll ever forgive her. People only call me Melanie when they want to make me mad or get back at me for something. Usually I'm Mel. Mel Rosidis.

Jim smiled at Tammy-Ann – all men smile at Tammy-Ann – and she simpered back at him. 'Good morning,

Jim,' she said.

I slumped down in the empty chair next to Danny Angeleno and tried to pretend I was somewhere else. Anywhere else. Preferably somewhere warm, where it never rained. Honolulu maybe. Or Casablanca. Athens. No, my father lived in Greece. Somewhere else. Peru. Anywhere that was a long way away from Jim Curtis and Tammy-Ann Ziegler and Chalfont.

Jim was talking about *Macbeth* and I let his words wash over me as I looked round the room. Classes at Chalfont are small – there are fourteen of us doing Eng. Lit. – and informal. No rows of desks here: we sit round in a circle. Some people think that Chalfont carries informality too far; there's no school uniform, for instance, and we can come and go pretty much as we please in the fifth and sixth forms, provided we attend all our classes. Parents tend to be alarmed by the fact that we call the teachers by their first names but that's one of the Chalfont traditions. *And* one of the most civilised things about the place. The students aren't too bad, either, though there are some exceptions. Tammy-Ann Ziegler for one, and Super-Nerd Jay Hendriksen, who always looks like an unmade bed. His father's a big shot in a multi-national oil company and they moved here from Australia. Jay Hendriksen is living proof that not all Australians are big, bronzed, and beautiful.

About half our class and most of the school are from other countries. We all *live* in London, of course, but a lot of our parents move around a good deal which is why they prefer the international education that Chalfont offers. Gorgeous Gary Goldman's father is something in the

United States Embassy, for instance; the Goldmans moved here from Moscow and could be moved on again at any moment. Abby Skarbnik's mother is an actress and spends half her time in America. Lee Nelson's father is the ambassador of one of the Caribbean countries – I forget which one. Some of us live in London all the time, though. Laura Cordell, for instance, and me. But most Chalfont students are only here for a while. It was an exciting place to be because of that. But not on a wet Monday morning.

Olivia Strickland was talking now. Olivia's the only person I know who can look intelligent at nine-fifteen in the morning. She seemed to know a great deal about *Macbeth* and I remembered my half-finished essay and shuddered. Jim Curtis was gazing thoughtfully at the ceiling; he was probably as bored as the rest of us. Next to me, Danny Angeleno seemed to be asleep. I studied him surreptitiously. No one would ever guess that Danny was sixteen years old, the same age as the rest of us; his red hair and button nose and freckles made him look twelve at the most. Rather like Mickey Rooney in those old musicals with Judy Garland.

I looked idly past Danny and then my jaw dropped in surprise. There was a stranger in the class. In the chair next to Danny was sitting a boy I'd never seen before in my life. Someone new. And what a someone! The stranger had wavy black hair and the sultriest pair of dark eyes I've ever seen in my life; they were staring at Olivia Strickland in a puzzled way, as though he had no idea what on earth she was talking about. He should join the club, I thought glumly. No one knows what Olivia is talking about most of the time. She has more brains than the rest of us put together.

I gave Danny a nudge. 'Who's that next to you?' I hissed. 'And what's his phone number?'

Danny shot me a grin. 'If you'd been on time you'd know,' he whispered back. 'Anthony Something. No, Anton. From South America somewhere.'

'South America?' I was impressed. Anton Something was staring at the floor now, finally defeated by Olivia Strickland's views on the madness of Lady Macbeth. He looked depressed and I didn't blame him. To be plunged into Eng. Lit. at nine-fifteen on a wet British Monday morning is no joke, believe me.

'And what do *you* think, Melanie? Do you agree with Olivia's point about Macbeth's feelings of guilt?'

I looked quickly away from the mysterious stranger to meet Jim Curtis's mocking gaze.

'Well, er – um – I think – well, um –' I stammered, and then said lamely, 'I didn't actually get the point she was trying to make.'

'Perhaps you'd better repeat it for Melanie's benefit, Olivia,' Jim said. 'On second thoughts, don't. We don't want to waste everyone else's time.'

I glared at him, and looked quickly away. It didn't look as though this Monday was going to improve. So far it had been one disaster after another.

I shot a glance at Anton Something. He was looking straight at me with those dark velvet eyes. He gave me a sympathetic smile and I beamed back. It seemed as though I wasn't the only person in the class who didn't understand what on earth Olivia Strickland was talking about.

At long last the class ended and we all scrambled for the door. Danny and Anton Something headed down the corridor together and I was just about to follow them when Jim called me back.

'I'd like your essay, Mel, if it's ready,' he said.

My heart sank into my shoes and I turned slowly to face him. Now for it. He'd called me Mel and not Melanie, which was a good omen, but he'd be back with the longer version when he heard the glad tidings about my essay.

'I – I haven't quite finished it,' I confessed. 'It'll be ready tomorrow, I promise.'

Jim looked annoyed. 'Well, let's hope so,' he said. 'The others have finished theirs. I collected them before class today. You really must learn to hand assignments in on time.'

I shuffled my feet nervously. I felt about two inches tall. Rules are very relaxed at Chalfont and senior students especially are trusted to get on with their work without threats of detention or other punishments. We know that we're the losers if work isn't done.

'I'm sorry,' I muttered. 'Things are a bit tough right now . . .' My voice tailed off miserably.

'You're a good student, Mel,' Jim said. 'Don't waste your chances.'

I forced a smile. 'No, I won't. And thanks. I'll give you the essay tomorrow.' Then, swinging the conversation round to a much more interesting topic, 'Who's the new man? I missed the introductions.'

Jim gathered his books from a table and we walked to the door together. 'Oh, Anton Velasco. He joined Chalfont today.'

8

'Danny told me he's from South America,' I said, fishing for information.

'That's right,' said Jim. 'Venezuela, I believe. His English isn't too bad but he'll find things tough at first. I've asked Danny to take him under his wing for the next few days but I hope you'll all help him feel at home.'

Just give me a half a chance, I thought. But I said, 'Venezuela? Where the oil comes from?'

'That's right. But don't look too hopeful, Mel. I doubt if Anton's an oil tycoon.'

'I'll let you know,' I said sweetly, and sailed past him out of the room.

By that time I was late for my next class and so I didn't catch up with Danny and Anton until lunch-time when I saw them heading down the drive, together with Tammy-Ann Ziegler and Abby Skarbnik. Trust Tammy-Ann to get in on the act, I thought, and galloped in pursuit. I caught up with them just as they reached the gates.

'Oh, hi, Mel,' Danny said when he saw me. 'We're going to Gino's. Coming?'

Gino's is a hamburger place in Acacia Road that we go to whenever we can't face the school cafeteria. Catering is not one of Chalfont's strengths. Danny dropped back to walk with me, while the other three walked on ahead. Anton looked great from behind. He was wearing a pale jacket over a jade green sweater, and dark cord trousers. He looked a bit too smart to be a Chalfont student but he'd learn. By the end of the week he'd look as sloppy as the rest of us. I tried to work out how I could get to walk next to him but it wasn't going to be easy: Tammy-Ann was

9

sticking to him like glue.

As we turned the corner into Acacia Road, I glanced back towards the school. A man was following behind us, a dark-haired man in a black raincoat. I didn't think anything of it at the time – after all, London is crowded with dark-haired men in black raincoats – but there was a watchful anxiety about him that made me give him a second look. But then we reached Gino's and I turned my attention to the interesting task of getting a seat next to Anton.

It wasn't easy but I managed it. I pushed in front of Tammy-Ann and slipped into the booth next to Anton before she realised what was happening. Then, not to be outdone, she sat down right opposite him, where she could look straight into those velvet eyes. Danny and Abby squeezed in beside her. You could see that Abby wasn't much interested in Anton; all her thoughts were concentrated on tomorrow's auditions for *Our Town*. Abby's the school stage star but that's hardly surprising when you realise that she's Maxine Anderson's daughter. Yes, *the* Maxine Anderson.

We ordered hamburgers and Cokes and then I turned to Anton. 'I hope you're settling in okay,' I said, trying to sound more nonchalant than I felt.

'Yes. Is very good here, I think.' His voice was as dark as his eyes.

'I hear you're from Venezuela?'

'Yes. From Venezuela.'

Anton may have had a sexy voice but he was no great shakes at conversation. Still, it was his first morning at a new school in a strange country. It was only to be expected

10

that he'd be shy at first.

'I've always wanted to go to South America,' I said. 'It must be very beautiful.'

Anton gave me a slow sad smile. 'It *is* beautiful,' he said softly. 'Very beautiful. I wish you could – '

And then Tammy-Ann broke in with a long and boring story about a holiday she'd once spent in Brazil, and I turned my attention to my hamburger.

It was then that I noticed the man in the black raincoat again. He'd followed us inside, and was sitting alone at a table near the door. There was a cup of coffee in front of him but he didn't seem to be paying it much attention. He seemed much more interested in us.

I turned to the others and lowered my voice dramatically. 'Hey, see that man by the door? I think he's following us.'

'Don't be theatrical, Mel,' Abby said coolly.

I glared at her. She was a fine one to talk. 'No, I mean it,' I said. 'I swear he followed us here from school.'

Danny turned to look at the man. 'Just coincidence,' he said. 'Why should anyone follow *us?*'

'Yeah!' screeched Tammy-Ann. 'Why should they?'

Anton said nothing. He was staring fixedly at the table as though it was the most interesting thing he'd ever seen in his life. And his face was a fascinating shade of pink.

Then Danny and Tammy-Ann started to talk about the new Woody Allen movie that she'd seen the night before, and I forgot about the man in the black raincoat for a while. But only for a while. When I looked up again, the table by the door was empty. I turned to Anton but he avoided my gaze and began to ask Abby a lot of boring questions about the Tower of London.

I got through the rest of that day somehow but there were more disasters before it ended. In Art, I knocked a jar of water all over Michelle Chan's tasteful pastel study of driftwood and roses, and then, because clearing up the mess made me late for History, I collided with the headmaster's secretary in the corridor and sent both her and her burden of assorted stationery flying in all directions.

'What a day!' I complained to Laura Cordell and Abby Skarbnik as we walked down to the gate when school was over. 'In future I'm going to stay in bed all day on Mondays.'

'Me too,' said Laura. She and Abby are cousins but you'd never guess it to look at them. Laura is slim and fair and subdued, while Abby is just the opposite. Today she had her dark curls tied up in a vivid scarlet scarf that made her look like a beautiful gipsy princess.

'Did you see anything more of that man who was following –' Abby began, and then she gripped my arm fiercely. 'Talk of the devil,' she said.

'What's the matter?' I said, and then gasped as I followed her gaze.

Parked on the road outside the school gate was a large black limousine with dark tinted windows. And there, standing beside it, was Anton Velasco, deep in conversation with the dark-haired man in the black raincoat. Then, as we watched open-mouthed, the man opened the rear door and helped Anton inside the car. He then walked round to the far side and got into the driver's seat. Slowly, silently, the car slid out of sight in the direction of Regent's Park.

Abby turned to me, her brown eyes alight with excitement. 'Well, then,' she said. 'What do you make of *that*?'

'I don't know,' I said blankly. 'I honestly don't know.'

CHAPTER TWO

Flanagan was crashing about in the kitchen when I let myself into the flat. She always makes a great deal of noise when she's cooking but I have to admit that the results are usually pretty good. I popped my head round the door and said, 'Hi!'

She was stirring something in a saucepan and didn't look up. 'Had a good day?' she said.

'You must be joking,' I growled, and headed for the refrigerator.

'I only asked,' she said. 'It's part of my job to be polite.'

'I'm sorry,' I said, regretting my bad temper. 'It's been a foul day. I'm sorry, okay?'

'Okay. Want me to get you anything?' She peered suspiciously into the saucepan. 'I don't think this can be right. It's turning *green*, for God's sake.'

'Maybe it's supposed to,' I suggested, as I rummaged in the fridge for anything that looked edible. 'Anyway, it'll taste good whatever colour it is.'

I was beginning to feel better already. Being with Flanagan always has that effect on me, and I think Theo feels the same way. Finding her was one of the best things my mother ever did. I suppose that Flanagan is really an au pair but she's much more of a mother to us than our real one is. She's always there when we need her, which is more than can be said for my mother. I once went for two whole weeks without seeing my mother at all, even though she was living in the apartment the whole time. Her job does take her away from us a lot, I know, but that's not really her fault. But I sometimes wonder if she doesn't go out of her way to avoid us. Flanagan's the next best thing, though. She came to London from Australia for a holiday sixteen years ago and has been here ever since. We call her Flanagan because she can't stand her first name. We've never been able to find out what it is, so Flanagan she has stayed. It doesn't suit her at all, because she's tall and slim, with short curly fair hair, brilliant blue eyes, and a warm flashing smile. She really deserves a much prettier name. I don't know what we'd do without her. At the back of my mind is the constant nagging fear that one of these days she'll decide to go home. Or get married or something. Mind you, she's thirty-two years old so there's not much chance of that.

I crossed the kitchen and gave her a quick hug. She looked at me in surprise and then turned back to her saucepan. 'I wonder if I'd better start again,' she said gloomily. 'Oh, your mother's out at an audition or something. She said she won't be back till late so don't wait up.'

I didn't say anything. It was the same old story. I only ever seem to see my mother at weekends. She gets up after I've left for Chalfont, and doesn't come back till I've gone to bed. Big deal. I might just as well be an orphan. At least I'd know then exactly where I stood. My father went back to Greece after the divorce and we never see him. The divorce was dreadful, a time of shouting and pain and hate, and I try not to think about it too much. My father wanted custody of Theo and me but he didn't get it. I know this hurt him terribly because he really wanted us. Especially Theo, his only son. But that all happened five years ago and we've learned to live without him.

I made myself a tunafish sandwich and poured a glass of milk. Then I headed for the sitting room in search of Theo. He was there as usual, slumped in front of the blaring television set. He only watches the commercial channels because there's always a chance that he'll see my mother. She's an actress. Not a famous star like Abby Skarbnik's mother, who acts for the Royal Shakespeare Company when she isn't making those movies with Walter Matthau. My mother acts in commercials and does voice-overs and gets small parts in television series if she's lucky. She was in some of the early James Bond pictures but she's too old for that sort of part now and her legs aren't what they were.

I joined Theo on the sofa. 'Any luck?'

'Not so far.' He's eight years old but small for his age. His hair is black like mine and he always looks neat. Unlike me. 'I'm hoping they'll show that shampoo commercial of hers again. It was on three times yesterday.'

'Oh no!' I groaned.

I hate that shampoo commercial, it's really embarrassing. You must have seen it. First of all, there's a fuzzy shot of my mother in a shower, but as it's a commercial you don't actually *see* anything, if you know what I mean. Then there's a close-up, all gleaming hair and about two hundred teeth, as she turns to the camera and says, 'It's not just because I'm an actress that I like to have beautiful hair, it's also because I'm a woman.' That's the point when

16

the entire nation throws up. My mother hates that advertisement too but not quite for the right reasons. She hates it because they used someone else's body for the fuzzy shower shot. Well, as I said, her legs aren't what they were.

I sat with Theo until the next commercial break and our patience was rewarded. They showed my mother's most recent catfood commercial, the one in which she says that she always feeds her prize tabby with whatever tinned muck it happens to be, I forget. Little does the audience realise that my mother is the world's number one cat hater. But she'll act in anything for money. Luckily, very few people know exactly who my mother is. I'd die if anyone at Chalfont found out that she's the woman in that shampoo commercial.

'Some new people have moved in upstairs,' Theo said after a while.

'Oh yes?' The flat above ours is the penthouse, an enormous apartment which stretches the full length of the building and has its own roof garden. I'd only been up there once, when the Lessmans, who used to live there, invited us to their housewarming party. The roof garden had real trees and grass and a fountain. I couldn't believe my eyes. Real trees growing seven floors above the street. I've never been able to work out why the roots don't force their way down to our apartment. Maybe they will, one day. My mother said that the garden and the apartment were really tacky but I think I could learn to live with that kind of tackiness. The place had been empty now for a couple of months.

'Have you seen the new people?' I asked Theo.

17

'I don't think so. Just their furniture and stuff.' He turned his attention back to the screen. A woman with bright red hair was telling us how to keep our hands soft and lovely after doing the washing-up. I pulled a face at her and went on to the balcony.

The balcony is the best thing about our apartment. It runs half the length of the building – there are only two apartments on each floor – and there's plenty of room for plants and furniture and sunbathing, whenever there's any sun to bathe in. We're on the sixth floor, with only the penthouse above us, but even so there's not much of a view. If you lean over the balcony railing and peer to the right, you can just about see the trees in Regent's Park but, apart from that, all there is to look at are the other blocks of flats in our part of St John's Wood. The nearest building to ours is Park Plaza; we're so close that it sometimes feels as though one could just lean over and shake hands with the people in the apartments on the same level as ours. Actually, the buildings are about fifty yards apart separated by the back gardens of each block, but it seems as though they're much closer. And the apartments aren't really on the same level; Park Plaza is on slightly higher ground so that the top floor is on a level midway between our floor and the penthouse.

I didn't spend too much time watching the flats in the opposite block, mainly because there wasn't too much to see. Like our building, there were two apartments on each floor. One of the top apartments was occupied by an elderly couple and several cats, all of whom seemed to spend the greater part of each day asleep; the other flat on the top floor seemed to be empty. At least, I'd never seen any sign of life there. Tammy-Ann Ziegler lived on the first floor but she kept well out of my way, I'm glad to say. Apart from her, I didn't know any of the people who lived in Park Plaza and all I could see were six floors of identical anonymous net-curtained windows.

I sank into a chair with the remains of my sandwich and thought about that awful Monday. The only bright spot had been the arrival of the mysterious Anton and the even more mysterious man in the black raincoat. Who on earth were they? It was going to be interesting finding out. In the meantime, though, there was that *Macbeth* essay to finish. I sighed, and wished that I was better friends with Olivia Strickland. Maybe I should give her a call . . .

I gazed idly across at Park Plaza, and then sat up with a jerk. The building looked different. Something had changed. It was a couple of minutes before I realised exactly what the difference was: there was someone in the empty flat on the top floor. The net curtains at one of the windows had been pulled aside, and someone was standing there, looking out. Looking at our building. There was someone there, watching.

The watcher was a woman. She stood quite still, staring across at our block. She seemed to be looking very intently at the floor above ours. At the penthouse. I ducked my head instinctively but I don't think she could have seen me because she didn't move away from the window as people do when they know they've been seen looking out. The woman stood at the window without moving, staring, watching.

I felt a sudden twinge of fear. There was something sinister about that silent figure staring so intently at the flat upstairs. What could she see? What was she looking at? Who was up there?

Then there was a sudden shout from the sitting room behind me. 'Quick, Mel, it's Mum! The shampoo commercial!'

I got up and ran inside, glad of an excuse to forget the watcher. And later, when I'd seen my mother praising her shampoo for the umpteenth time and went back to the balcony to fetch my empty plate and glass, the watcher had vanished. All I could see now were the blank curtained windows, grey and lifeless like sightless eyes.

CHAPTER THREE

I didn't sleep very well that night. Every time I shut my eyes, I saw again that strange silent watcher, staring, staring at the floor above ours. Who was she? The woman had looked harmless enough: grey-haired and elderly, with glasses. But there was something frightening about the intensity of her stare, and the memory of it kept me awake for long hours that night. And, because I hadn't been able to get to sleep, I didn't hear my alarm in the morning, and so I was late *again*.

At least I'd finished the *Macbeth* assignment, sort of, and Jim Curtis wouldn't have anything to complain about this time. I'd finished the essay the night before, after supper. And after that I'd given Abby a call because I felt uneasy about the watcher and needed to talk to someone who wasn't an eight-year-old brother.

I like Abby Skarbnik more than anyone else in our class at Chalfont. We're very different in some ways – I'm not as lively or attractive as she is, and I'm more nervous with people I don't know – but we get on very well most of the time. Abby had been feeling miserable last night. For one thing, her relationship with Gary Goldman was going through a bad patch, as usual. And for another, she was in a state of terror about the next day's auditions for *Our Town*.

Abby had been going out with Gary Goldman for years – well, two terms at least. I couldn't understand what she saw in him. To misquote the song, Gary was lovely to look at but lousy to know. Maybe, to quote the song again, it was because he was also heaven to kiss that Abby kept going out with him when any other girl in her right mind would have given him the elbow months ago. Gary is arrogant and selfish and vain, and those are just his good points. He was the one thing that Abby and I agreed to differ about; mind you, she hadn't liked Jordan much, either, so that made us even. Maybe it's usual for best friends to hate each other's boyfriends. I don't know. All I *do* know is that if a boy treated me the way Gary Goldman treated Abby Skarbnik, then he wouldn't see me for dust.

Last night on the phone, Abby had been upset because Gary hadn't kept a date they'd made after school. And then, when she'd droned on about that for half an hour, I had to listen to her worries about the *Our Town* auditions. Mind you, it's not easy for her, being Maxine Anderson's daughter. There'd be no problem if Abby wanted to be a brain surgeon or an astronaut. But she wanted to be an actress like her mother, and that complicated things. Whenever she was given a part in a play, Abby could never be sure whether she'd been cast because she was a good actress or because she was Maxine Anderson's daughter. And she was terrified of failure on stage. She felt certain that everyone expected her to be a brilliant actress just because her mother was.

I didn't say anything to Abby about the strange watcher in the opposite block. I thought about telling her while she was yammering on about Gorgeous Gary Goldman but I

22

decided against it. After all, there wasn't much to tell. I had seen an elderly woman looking out of a window. There was nothing odd about that. There was no law against looking out of windows. She hadn't been doing anything wrong. She had been simply standing at a window, that's all. Watching. So I decided not to tell Abby. Not yet, anyway. Instead, we talked about Anton Velasco and whether he was as mysterious and fascinating as he looked. I decided that he wasn't but Abby was prepared to give him the benefit of the doubt. I think we both felt more cheerful when at last Flanagan dragged me away from the phone.

It was only when I got into bed and switched out the light that the anxiety returned and I remembered the strange silent figure at the window. And then, when at last I fell asleep, I dreamed that I was being chased down a long corridor by a little old lady who looked just like Gary Goldman.

That Tuesday morning was a repeat performance of the day before. I was late and it was raining. The only noticeable difference was that Theo didn't throw up all over the kitchen floor the minute I walked in. This time, he didn't even bother to look up from his bowl of muesli when I staggered into the kitchen in search of something to eat on the way.

'You're late,' Flanagan said. She was sitting at the table, munching toast.

I glared at her as I grabbed a couple of apples from the bowl on the fridge.

'Aren't you having any breakfast?' she went on. 'You should eat something.'

'No time,' I said. 'I'm late, as you so kindly reminded me.'

Flanagan opened her mouth to say something and then, seeing the expression on my face, changed her mind and shut it again. Instead, she pointed to an envelope lying on the table. An air-mail envelope. Could it possibly . . .

'For me?' I said.

Flanagan nodded and I snatched it up. I stared at the familiar writing, hardly able to believe my eyes. A letter from Jordan. I knew he'd write. He hadn't forgotten me. He still cared. A letter at last. A letter from Jordan.

'Didn't you say you were late?' Flanagan smiled. 'It's quarter past.'

'Oh no!' I stuffed the letter into my bag and headed for the kitchen door.

'See you later!' she shouted after me as I banged my way into the hall and out of the apartment.

As I waited for the elevator to arrive, I checked to make sure I hadn't forgotten anything. Essay, books, cash for lunch, pen, Jordan's letter . . . I knew I looked a mess but there was nothing I could do about that. I made a mental note to buy a louder alarm clock on the way home.

There was a ping as the elevator arrived from the floor above. The doors slid open and I rushed inside, reaching instinctively for the ground floor button. It wasn't until the doors had closed again that I realised someone else was in the lift. I turned to look, and my jaw dropped in amazement. The other person in the lift was – Anton Velasco!

I think that he was just as surprised as I was. We gaped at each other like two startled goldfish as the lift began to

24

descend. What on earth was he doing there? In *my* lift at that time of the morning!

And then the penny dropped with a deafening clunk. I remembered yesterday afternoon and Theo saying, 'Some people have moved in upstairs.' Of course. The new people in the penthouse must be Anton Velasco and – who?

I grinned at him like an idiot and then said, 'Hi! Fancy meeting you!'

He smiled nervously, and took a step backwards. 'Good morning,' he said. 'I did not know –' His voice tailed away to nothing, as though he'd suddenly forgotten every word of English he knew. Maybe he had. What language did they speak in Venezuela? Spanish? I suddenly wished that I'd chosen Spanish as my second language instead of French.

'I'm so late,' I said nervously. 'It's the second morning in a row that I haven't heard the alarm, and it's raining again, and the last person I expected to see –' Anton was staring at me as though I was the Creature from the Black Lagoon. I must look a mess, I thought. I'd flung on the first clothes I'd come across. And my hair . . . I hadn't touched my hair. I must look *dreadful*. And then I began to gabble, as I always do when I'm nervous. 'I guess you've moved into the penthouse. I mean, they say it's a small world but *really*, to think you've been living right over my head and I'd no idea, none whatsoever . . .'

It was dreadful. I knew I was talking nonsense. I knew that utter gibberish was pouring out of my mouth but there was nothing I could do to stop it. The more I tried to shut up, the more stupid I sounded. Anton was staring at

25

me in horror; he must have thought I was out of my mind.
'. . . and I really thought that the man in the black raincoat was following you, a kidnapper or something, I don't know, but then when I saw the two of you together, well, I didn't know *what* to think because – ' And then I had to stop talking as the lift came to a halt on the ground floor.

Anton dashed out into the lobby as though his life depended on it.

'Hang on!' I shouted. 'Anton, wait! Can't we – '

And then my jaw dropped in amazement for the second time that morning. The dark man in the black raincoat was waiting by the entrance. When he saw Anton coming towards him, he immediately opened one of the heavy glass doors. Anton walked straight past him without saying a word and headed towards the large black limousine that was parked outside. As he climbed into the back of the car, the raincoat man hurried after him and got into the driver's seat. It was only when the limousine had slid away from the kerb and was heading in the direction of Prince Albert Road that I realised what had happened.

'You creeps!' I yelled. 'You might at least have given me a lift!'

I stared angrily into the rain and then turned and plonked myself down on one of the sofas that lined the lobby.

Old Cocky Nose popped his head out of his cubby-hole and peered at me curiously. 'Shall I ring for a taxi, miss?' he asked.

Old Cocky Nose is the porter of our building, in charge of maintenance and security and that sort of thing. He's good at his job; a bit too good, if you ask me. Nothing and

26

no one can get into that lobby without him knowing about it.

'No thanks, Mr Kokkinos,' I said sweetly. 'I guess the rain'll stop soon.'

Old Cocky Nose sniffed gloomily. 'I wouldn't count on it,' he said, and retreated into his office.

I stared at the rain for a while and then I remembered Jordan's letter. This would be a good time to read it. I was going to be late anyway, so another five minutes wouldn't make any difference. I fished the envelope out of my bag and slit it open with my thumbnail.

There was a single sheet of thin blue paper inside. Big deal, I thought. Still, a short letter was better than nothing at all. I'd waited long enough for this one. I unfolded the sheet and read:

> *Dear Mel,*
>   *Sorry I haven't written for so long but you know how it is, there's so much to do and not enough hours in the day.*

No, Jordan, I thought. I don't know how it is. I spend most of my time wondering why you haven't written to me, dumdum.

> *It's great to be back in New Hampshire. Nothing much happens in Concord but we get into Manchester or Boston once in a while for a good time. I'm looking forward to college – it'll be good to be part of a larger community again.*

Who's we?

I often think of you and my time in England. How are the folks at Chalfont? Say hello to Gary and Abby and Danny for me. If they remember me.

How could they forget? I keep whining on about you. They must be sick of the sound of your name.

We're planning a trip –

We again.

– to the West Coast this summer. We'll stay in California for a time and then maybe work our way down thru Mexico and points south. We may end up in Venezuela, who knows?

Venezuela. Venezuela. Suddenly everything's Venezuela. First Anton, now Jordan. We'd planned a trip of our own this summer, Jordan and I. We were going to hike through France and on into Italy. I'd never been to Rome. I'd always wanted to visit the Colosseum and the Sistine Chapel, and we were going to see them together. Now Jordan was going to Venezuela with – who? And I was going nowhere. All by myself.

Then it's back to good old N.H. and college in the fall. Did I tell you I've got into Dartmouth?

No, you didn't. You haven't told me anything since February.

> *Maybe I'll get over to Europe sometime in the summer*
> *if California doesn't work out. My folks send their*
> *regards.*

Jordan's father was a professor of English Literature.
He'd been teaching at London University before he was
offered a job at a New Hampshire college and took Jordan
back with him to the States.

> *Say 'Hi' to your mom and to Teddy for me.*

Teddy? *Theo*, not Teddy. The slug can't even remember
the name of my kid brother.

> *Write soon and let me know how you're doing.*
> *Yours, Jordan.*

And that was all. *That* was the letter I'd been hoping for
and praying for since February. That was all he could be
bothered to write.

I crumpled the thin blue sheet into a tight ball and threw
it as hard as I could across the lobby. It bounced against
the elevator doors and rolled into a corner. Old Cocky
Nose would go berserk when he saw it; he liked his lobby
to be spotless. I peered outside. It was still raining, and I
felt as miserable as the weather.

Jordan didn't care about me any more. I knew that for
certain now. But what had I expected? *Dear Mel, I love you*
madly. Will you marry me? Or, *Dearest Mel, I can't live*

29

without you. I'm coming back to London next week? No, I hadn't expected that sort of letter. I hadn't *wanted* that sort of letter. I'd just expected – a little bit more, that's all. All I'd really wanted was a message to say that our time together had been important, was *still* important, and that Jordan missed me as much as I missed him. But his letter showed that he didn't care any more. Maybe he'd never really cared. Anyway, I was no longer a part of his life. His life now was New Hampshire and college and trips to Venezuela.

Venezuela.

I jumped to my feet as I remembered where I was and where I was supposed to be going. Thanks to Anton Velasco and Jordan Macdonald, I was late, late, *late*.

I grabbed my bag and hurtled through the doors into the spring rain.

CHAPTER FOUR

Luckily, History was the first class that morning so I didn't have to make excuses to Jim Curtis two days in a row. Anton was sitting at the far side of the room with Danny, and he had the grace to blush and look away when I glared in his direction. He wasn't in English, for some reason, and so he missed the flamboyant curtsey I gave Jim Curtis when I handed him my *Macbeth* essay. Jim opened his mouth to say something – a witty remark about essays being better late than never, I expect – but he took one look at my face and muttered, 'Thanks, Mel,' instead.

After that I endured forty minutes of Conversational French before coming to a rest under the oaks at the far side of the games field. I often take shelter there when I want to be alone at break time, and so it didn't take Abby long to find me.

'Hi!' she said, flopping down beside me on the grass. 'I've been trying to catch up with you all morning. What's got into you, Mel?'

I took a large bite out of my breakfast apple before replying. Abby was my greatest friend and there was no reason why she should suffer from my bad temper.

'Just one of those days, I guess,' I said.

Abby didn't say anything. That's one of the things I like most about her: she knows when to keep quiet.

After a while I said, 'What happened to Latin Lover this morning? He was in History but I didn't see him after that.'

'Who?'

'Anton Velawhatsit. You *know*, the new –'

'Oh, *him*. The one with the eyes. Danny says they've reorganised his courses or something. He's doing English as a Foreign Language now instead.'

'Just wait till I get my hands on him,' I said darkly.

'Ooh, nice!' Abby giggled.

'Not like that, you toad,' I laughed, and went on to tell her about our meeting in the lift that morning and how Anton had driven off without me.

'Well, maybe he thought you were going by car, too,' Abby said. 'How was he to know you used the bus?'

There are times when Abby Skarbnik drives me mad with rage. She always gives people the benefit of the doubt and I was in no mood then for discovering Anton Velasco's good points, if he had any. As far as I was concerned, he was a rude and selfish creep and if I never saw him again it would be too soon.

'Anyway,' Abby said when I'd told her all this, 'why waste your bad temper on *him*. Think of someone more worthwhile.'

'I have,' I muttered. 'I had a letter from Jordan this morning.'

'From Jordan! Oh, Mel, I know how much you –' She stopped short when she saw my face. 'Not a good letter?' she suggested cautiously.

I shook my head. 'One page of very big handwriting.' Then, 'And don't tell me that's better than nothing,' I added quickly before Abby had time to open her mouth. 'He managed to say precisely nothing at all. Nothing important, anyway. Except that he and some mysterious *someone* are going to California this summer and on down to Mexico and – and other places.'

'Lucky them.'

'But we were going to France together this summer. We'd *planned* it all. We –'

Abby put her hand on my arm but I shook it off. 'He didn't say a word about that,' I went on angrily. 'He didn't say a word about *us*. Just – just – just *nothing*.'

'Come off it, Mel.' There was a note of impatience in Abby's voice now. 'You planned that trip before he left. Before he knew he was going back to the States. Surely you didn't think that it would still go ahead?'

Of course I didn't. I knew that perfectly well. Abby was right, as usual. She was always right.

'Anyway,' she went on, 'his parents wouldn't have allowed him to go. Neither would your mother.'

'He's going to California,' I mumbled.

'That's what he *says*. Maybe he is. Maybe he isn't.' She put her arm around my shoulders and this time I didn't shrug it off. 'Forget about Jordan, Mel. He just isn't worth it. He never was.'

The bell for the next class rang then. I stood up and turned to help Abby to her feet.

'Thanks, Abby,' I said. 'I feel better for that. Though I'd still like to murder that slob Velasco,' I added viciously.

'Agony Auntie Abby always at your service,' she said as we started back towards the school. 'And now it's your turn.'

'My turn?'

'Come and keep me company at the *Our Town* auditions this lunch-time.'

'Okay, but I can't imagine what you're worried about. You'll get a part without even trying. You know you're the best actress at Chalfont.'

Abby stopped dead. 'But I want to play Emily,' she wailed. 'And I don't *look* right.'

'So how does Emily look?' I asked. 'Does it say in the script what she looks like?'

Abby considered. 'No, it doesn't. I'm sure it doesn't. But I *know* I'm wrong for it. She should be small and fair not dark and lumpy like me.'

Now it was my turn to get impatient. 'Oh, come off it, Abby. You know you'll get the part.'

'But what if I *don't*?'

'What does it matter? It's only a play, for crying out loud.'

'Only a play!' Abby was indignant. 'It's only one of the greatest plays ever written. It's only –'

'Oh, shut up!' I laughed, and ran on ahead towards the peace and quiet of Biology and Art.

Abby and I met up again at lunchtime. We gobbled a quick salad in the cafeteria – or rather, *I* gobbled a quick salad because Abby claimed to be too nervous to eat a thing – and then we headed for the theatre together.

Chalfont is very proud of the school theatre. It's not just a glorified hall but a proper auditorium with a fully-equipped stage and raked seating. My mother says that it's far better equipped than most of the professional theatres

34

she's played in. The building was donated years ago by a famous actor whose children were at Chalfont and there's been a strong theatrical tradition at the school ever since. Critics from the national press often come to see our productions, and there's always a chance that theatrical agents and talent scouts will be in the audience.

The auditions had already started by the time we arrived. I sat down near the back of the theatre while Abby went to the front to speak to the producer, Maggie Farrell. Maggie is Head of Drama and famous for her bad temper. Not that there was much evidence of it that afternoon. In fact, the auditions were so boring that I almost fell asleep. I grew so bored at hearing the same speeches from *Our Town* over and over again that I actually decided to audition for a part myself. Tammy-Ann Ziegler was trying for one and I knew I couldn't be any worse than she was. Abby was by far the best, of course, and we all knew that she'd get the part of Emily even though Maggie Farrell said that she wouldn't make her final decision until the following week.

'How can she make us wait so long?' Abby groaned, as we walked down the drive together when school was over for the day. 'The suspense'll kill me. What does she think I'm made of? Stone?'

'You're not the only one who'll be waiting,' I reminded her. 'You're not the only one who wants to play Emily. And what about the rest of the cast? Other people auditioned too, you know.'

She stopped and looked at me in surprise. 'But you only read a part for fun, didn't you? You're not really serious about being in the play.'

'Aren't I? What makes you think that?'

For once, Abby was lost for words. Come to think of it, I was pretty surprised myself. Up until that moment, I hadn't taken the play at all seriously. Suddenly it seemed the most important thing in the world.

Then, just as suddenly, I forgot all about it as we came in sight of the school gates. Anton Velasco, looking devastating in cream trousers and a pale blue jacket, was leaning nonchalantly against one of the gateposts. A few yards past him, the black limousine was parked. The man in the black raincoat was leaning against it, looking cross.

Anton noticed me at the same moment as I saw him. He took a step towards me and then stopped. I didn't. Instead, I turned to Abby and asked her some idiotic question about our next History assignment, and we sailed through the gates without giving Anton a second glance. I didn't exactly stalk past him with my nose in the air – that would have been too Anne of Green Gables for words – but that was the effect I was aiming at.

'He was waiting for you,' Abby hissed as we paused on the pavement.

I didn't turn round to see. 'Don't be stupid,' I said. 'Why should he be waiting for me? Anyway, I don't want to see him, the creep.' I hesitated, and then said, 'What's he doing now?'

Abby peered over my shoulder. 'Nothing much. He's looking a bit lost. I think he's waiting for me to go.'

'No, don't, you mustn't!' I yelped, and grabbed Abby by the arm.

She laughed, and pushed my hand away. 'Don't be such a moron, Mel. Anyway, he's rather dishy. You could do worse.'

I agreed with her but I wasn't going to say so. 'Look,' I said, 'come home with me. We can go over that History together and –'

'Sorry. I'm seeing Gary at seven.' She looked at her watch. 'I must go, Mel. See you.' And she set off briskly in the direction of Swiss Cottage.

'Bye!' I called feebly, and started walking in the opposite direction. Slowly.

After a moment or two I heard footsteps behind me. I didn't turn round but increased my pace slightly and waited for him to say something. I knew Anton was following me. At least, I *hoped* Anton was following me. Maybe I was wrong. Maybe he *had* been waiting for someone else. I slowed down and resisted the temptation to look round.

'Melanie! Melanie, stop! Please!'

I stopped and turned. Anton was standing behind me, looking embarrassed. I gave him a long, cold stare.

'Melanie, I want to ask you.' His voice was as deep and sultry as I had remembered. 'Please, let me give you a lift in the car.'

I tried to look as icy as I could, but it wasn't easy. I could feel my legs growing weaker every second.

'I'm sorry for this morning,' Anton went on. 'For not talking and for running to car. It was very rude, I know. I apologise. Very much.'

Anton's accent was fascinating. He sounded just like a South American gigolo in an old Hollywood musical. And, as I looked into his large dark eyes, my legs began to wobble.

Oh God, I thought. I don't believe it. I knew I should

say no. I knew I should give him a withering stare, announce curtly that my mother had told me never to get into cars with strange men, and then turn on my heel and stride forcefully to my bus stop. I knew exactly what I should have done. Instead, I shuffled my feet nervously, grinned like a cretin, and said, 'May as well.'

The man in the black raincoat gave me a look of unconcealed contempt as he helped me into the car. I sank into the seat and wondered why he seemed so resentful. Perhaps Anton would say something about it. But he said nothing at all as he climbed in beside me and the car slid away from the kerb.

'Makes a change from the bus, anyway,' I said, and turned to look at Anton. His eyelashes were very long, and the skin on his high cheekbones was smooth and golden. My legs were like jelly and my heart started to pound.

'It was a big surprise to know you live in the same building,' Anton said. 'I'm sorry I not give you a lift. I was much surprised to see you.'

'Me, too,' I said, and laughed nervously.

'That's why I not offer lift,' he went on. 'I forget my manners.'

'Oh, think nothing of it,' I said loftily, and turned to look at him again. It was the long lashes that made his eyes seem so dark and lustrous, I decided. Then the eyes met mine and I looked quickly away and stared at the road ahead. I glanced at the driving mirror and saw reflected there the sullen gaze of the driver, the man in the black raincoat. *His* eyes were like small black stones.

I nudged Anton and whispered, 'Who *is* that?' He looked puzzled, and I went on, 'The man driving the car.

Who is he?'

Anton looked at me mischievously. 'The man driving the car. That is who he is.'

'Oh, very amusing,' I hissed frostily. 'But who *is* he? I mean, can you trust him?'

'I not know what you mean.'

'Can you trust him?' I repeated. 'He was following you yesterday. He seems to follow you everywhere you go.'

Anton looked puzzled for a moment and then let out a bellow of laughter. He leaned forward, tapped the driver on the shoulder, and gabbled at him in what I assume was Spanish. It sounded sharper and more staccato than the soft language I'd heard in Aragon last summer. Maybe the Venezuelan version was different. Anton laughed again but the driver didn't. His eyes met mine again in the mirror; he looked as stony and unfriendly as ever.

'Well, I'm glad I've caused you some amusement,' I said loftily.

'I'm sorry,' Anton said. 'It was not meant to be unkind. But is funny you think Carlos is following me.'

'Really? I don't see anything to laugh at.'

'No, is really funny,' Anton persisted. 'Carlos is my – how you say? – protector. He *must* follow me. Always.'

'A bodyguard, you mean?' I couldn't believe my ears. Why should Anton need a bodyguard?

'Carlos stays with me at all times,' Anton explained. 'When I am outside, of course. Not everywhere inside. Not in school, for instance. And not in other places. But look, here we are back once more.'

The car drew to a smooth halt outside our building and Carlos leaped out and opened the door for me. Then he followed Anton and me into the lobby.

'Which floor are you?' Anton asked as he pressed the button for the elevator.

'Sixth.'

'Ah,' he smiled. 'I am above you. In the – attic.'

'Penthouse,' I said.

He looked puzzled. 'Not attic? I thought attic is the word for rooms at the top of a house.'

'Yes, it is,' I said, 'but it's not really –'

Just then the lift arrived and I was saved the trouble of explaining why Anton's luxury penthouse could not by any stretch of the imagination be described as an attic. Carlos followed us into the lift and I could feel his disapproving gaze on me as we were carried upwards.

When the doors opened at my floor, I turned impulsively to Anton. 'Why don't you come in for a coffee or something?'

I regretted the suggestion the minute I'd made it. What on earth would he think? Apart from anything else, I didn't even like him. He might be smooth and good-looking and altogether desirable but he was still an arrogant creep. Still, my curiosity was stronger than my dislike. I wanted to know more about him. I wanted to know why he needed a bodyguard. Only people in movies had bodyguards. Apart from royalty and presidents, of course. But they were different, they were important. Kids at Chalfont didn't need bodyguards, surely.

Anton and Carlos were talking together now in Spanish. Carlos looked angry and I guessed that he didn't approve of my invitation. At last Anton turned back to me with a grimace and said, 'Thank you. You are most kind. I will

40

come.'

Carlos said something else, rather more loudly this time, and followed us out of the lift to the door of our apartment. I fished my key out of my bag and then turned to Anton.

'Look,' I said, 'I don't want seem rude but – er – your keeper or bodyguard or whatever isn't included in the invitation.'

Anton smiled sheepishly and shrugged. 'I'm sorry,' he said, 'but is all right. Carlos understands. He waits outside for me.'

I opened my mouth to protest and decided against it. Let him wait outside, if he wanted. It was nothing to do with me. I opened the door and led the way into the flat.

Flanagan and Theo were playing Scrabble in the sitting room when we walked in. The television set was mumbling away in the corner as usual; Theo didn't allow anything to divert him from mother-spotting, not even Scrabble with Flanagan. He was pretty good at the game, considering his age, but it was tough on Flanagan, having to play with him so often. I knew for a fact that she hated board games.

She stood up with relief when we came in. 'Hullo,' she said. 'Good day?'

I shrugged. 'This is Anton,' I said. 'He just moved in upstairs. He's at Chalfont, too.'

Theo looked up with interest at this. 'I saw them moving your furniture in,' he told Anton. 'Pretty fancy stuff.'

Anton shrugged and grinned. 'Just furniture,' he said. 'Things to live with for a while.'

For a while. So he wouldn't be staying long. Funny, no

41

one stayed anywhere for long. Sooner or later, everyone moved on. Moved away. Like Jordan.

'Can I get you two anything?' Flanagan asked. 'A Coke or something? There's apple pie, too, and some brownies I baked today.'

Flanagan bustled into the kitchen as Anton and I went out on to the balcony.

'A nice apartment,' he said politely. 'Your brother is cute. And your mother is very charming.'

I smiled at him and said, 'Flanagan's not my *mother*!' I explained who she was and what she did.

'Ah,' Anton said, his face brightening. 'She is like Carlos for you. And Josefina. Carlos and Josefina in one person. Very useful.'

'Josefina?'

'Carlos has wife, Josefina. He drives and, as you say, follows me. Josefina, she cooks and cleans in house. Upstairs.'

Aha, so there was a female Carlos, too. I wondered whether she was as miserable as he was.

'Your mother lives here?' Anton asked.

'Yes,' I said. 'She lives here. She's out at the moment, I expect.'

'And your father?'

'My father lives in Athens. My parents got divorced five years ago and we came to live here.'

'So you are Greek!' Anton looked strangely pleased with this discovery.

'Only half,' I pointed out. 'My mother's English, and I feel more English than anything else.'

'Have you lived in Greece?'

Why was he asking all these questions? My private life was nothing to do with him. He must have guessed then what I was thinking for he went on, 'Forgive me. I am just curious. People are interesting and I like to know about their lives.'

Yes, so do I, I thought. Especially those with body-guards.

'I lived in Athens when I was small,' I said. 'But we've moved around a lot. My father works for one of the big tanker companies. We've lived in France. And in America for a while, New York, Los Angeles. But since the divorce we've been in London.'

'Do you see your father still?'

Questions, more questions. I didn't want to talk about our family to him, but I said, 'I've been out to Greece to see him a couple of times. But my mother won't let Theo go.'

Flanagan appeared then with cold drinks and pie, and I looked at her thankfully. Maybe I'd be spared any further cross-examination for a while. While Anton showered Flanagan with compliments about her catering, I peered idly across at Park Plaza. And then, as I stared at the familiar balconies, I remembered the watcher of yester-day, the woman at the window staring at our building. At the apartment above.

Anton's apartment.

I stood up and walked to the balcony rail. Which was the watcher's window? Yes, there it was on the left-hand side. And then, as I looked, the net curtains were drawn aside and the face appeared. The face that I had seen the day before. The face of a grey-haired woman with glasses.

43

She stood at the window, watching. Staring. The woman and I looked at each other for a moment, and then the curtains dropped back into place and the face disappeared.

'Melanie? Are you all right?'

I turned. Flanagan had gone and Anton was looking at me curiously.

'Y-yes,' I stammered. 'I'm fine.' And then I felt I had to tell someone, anyone. 'There's a woman in a flat over there,' I said shakily. 'On the top floor. On the left. She keeps staring over here. At your flat.'

'At *my* flat?' Anton seemed to have grown pale, though it could have been my imagination. He stared across at Park Plaza.

'Yes,' I went on. 'I've seen her a couple of times now. Watching. She seems to be watching your flat.'

Anton put down his plate with a clatter. 'Nonsense,' he said. 'You are imagining things. There is no one watching. No one at all. It is your silly imagination.'

'I am *not* imagining it!' I said loudly. 'There is someone there. Someone *is* watching.'

Anton's face was white. He looked, somehow, frightened.

'There *is* someone watching your flat,' I repeated. 'I'm sure of it.'

'I do not believe you,' he said curtly. 'It is imagination. I can see nothing. Just curtains. Nothing.' He walked towards the sitting room and then turned and said stiffly, 'You are most kind but I must go now. I must go.' And he disappeared inside.

I stared after him, my mouth gaping like a stranded

44

fish. 'But you haven't finished your coke,' I called feebly. But he didn't come back.

And then my astonishment was replaced by anger. How dare he! How dare he walk off like that without saying anything? Who on earth did he think he was? One thing was certain, I'd been right all along. Anton Velasco was an arrogant creep. Like Jordan. Like the rest of them. I hated them all.

I stormed through the flat to my bedroom and slammed the door behind me. I never wanted to see Anton Velasco again. Ever.

CHAPTER FIVE

I calmed down after a while and came out of my room to have supper with the others and watch some television before getting down to my History. But I found it difficult to concentrate on the causes of World War One; I kept remembering the watcher in the opposite building and Anton's strange reaction when I'd told him. He'd certainly acted nervously for someone who didn't believe a word I was saying.

At about half past nine I finally gave up on World War One and went out to the sitting room. There was no one there. Theo had gone to bed and there was no sign of Flanagan. She was in her room, too, most probably. My mother was out; she'd left a note on the kitchen bulletin board to say that she was going to the National with Geraldine and then on to the Toreador with Morris Robinson and Jumbo, whatever that all meant, and that no one was to wait up for her. Too bad if the apartment caught fire or Flanagan had a heart attack or I was kidnapped. She'd never know. She'd be at the Toreador with Morris Robinson and Jumbo while the rest of us were rolling around in agony. Big deal. Maybe the watcher would sneak across and strangle us all in our beds. But she wouldn't do that, would she? It was Anton she was after. It was Anton she was watching. I felt sure of it now.

I crossed to the desk and found the pair of binoculars we kept there. Then I went to the glass doors that opened on to the balcony. Curtains were drawn across the doors but I didn't pull them back. Instead, I slipped between the pink velvet folds and opened the doors as quietly as I could. A chill wind whipped through my hair as I stepped out on to the balcony, and I shivered. Then I walked to the rail and stared across at Park Plaza.

The building looked quite different at night. During the day, all one could see were rows of windows, blinded with net. After dark, though, the windows sprang into life. Some remained obstinately dark, shrouded by curtains. But others sparkled with light and movement, with people sitting and watching television and eating and talking. The lighted windows looked just like miniature stage sets, one on top of the other, each one containing a real-life drama of its own. Every now and then, one of the actors would come to a window and draw curtains across to end the play.

By this time, only a few windows were uncurtained. I stared through the binoculars at the top floor. The windows there were in darkness. There was no way of telling if the flat was empty or not. There was no way of telling if the watcher was there in the dark. I pictured her standing alone, staring out towards me through a chink in the curtains. I shivered again, and not just with cold this time. Then I went back into the warmth and security of our flat and closed the doors firmly behind me. Before I went back into my room, I made sure that all the doors to the flat were firmly locked. Just in case.

Flanagan and Theo both looked surprised when I sat

down and joined them for breakfast next morning. For once, I hadn't overslept. In fact, I'd woken up before my alarm went off and had time to wash my hair before breakfast.

'Wonders will never cease,' Flanagan observed drily when she saw me.

'I'm turning over a new leaf,' I informed her.

Theo gave me a baleful stare. 'Who are you trying to kid?'

'Oh, shut up!' I laughed, and biffed him over the head with the cornflakes packet.

I left for Chalfont in good time. The last thing I wanted was to meet Anton in the lift again. I was still feeling angry with him, not just because he'd left the flat so abruptly the evening before but because he hadn't believed me when I'd told him about the watcher. He didn't exactly say that I was lying but he'd come pretty close to it. And I wasn't standing for that.

But I didn't see anything of Anton that morning. He seemed to be keeping out of my way: he sat as far away from me as he could in the one or two classes we shared, and he disappeared with Danny Angeleno and Jay Hendriksen at lunchtime. Abby and Gary Goldman seemed to have made up again after their recent bad patch and so I didn't see much of her either. In fact, the only company I had at break was Tammy-Ann Ziegler. Although I gave her no encouragement at all, she attached herself to me and spent twenty minutes screeching the praises of her new boyfriend. It seemed his name was Dane, so I'd been pretty close with my guess on Monday.

I didn't have any classes that afternoon and so, after an

hour's work in the library, I went home early. Apart from anything else, I didn't want to find Anton Velasco waiting for me at the gates with his Mercedes and his creepy bodyguard.

There was no one in when I got back to the flat. Flanagan was out, probably shopping before collecting Theo from school, and a note on the bulletin board that read 'Rehearsing. Back Late. M.' told me that I wouldn't be seeing much of my mother that day. I grabbed a coke from the fridge and wandered out on to the balcony. I stared at the familiar windows of Park Plaza. There was no movement anywhere, and the curtains at the watcher's windows remained undisturbed. Was she there in the rooms behind? Waiting and watching? I shuddered, and turned back into the flat and went to my room to do some work on the History assignment.

I worked on World War One for an hour or two. Every now and then I was interrupted by friendly afternoon sounds: a telephone ringing in the flat below, the faint hum of the elevator, the chatter of Theo and Flanagan coming home. Then the inevitable blare of the television as Theo settled down to watch commercials. It suddenly struck me that Theo didn't seem to have any friends; he rarely visited other kids' houses after school and I couldn't remember the last time he'd had a friend over at our place. He used to spend a lot of time with a boy who lived in the apartment below ours but that friendship ended when the family moved away last year. Occasionally Flanagan would cart him off to a birthday party or a movie but that was the limit of his social life. It wasn't right for a small boy to spend all his spare time watching television. He

49

should be out with friends, doing things. My mother should –

The doorbell rang. I sat up, and waited for Flanagan to answer it and then come and fetch me. It was bound to be for me; no one else had visitors.

I was right. After a minute or two, there was a knock at my door and Flanagan called, 'Mel! Someone to see you!'

'Coming!' I yelled back. It would be Abby, of course, come to tell me all about her great reconciliation with Gary Goldman. But I was in no mood for girlish talk about her love life. Or my lack of one.

But it wasn't Abby. When I came out of my room, I found Anton Velasco in the hall, peering intently at the old framed family photographs that my mother had grouped together on a wall by the front door. I was so surprised to see him that I stopped dead and gasped.

Anton turned to me, and grinned. 'You were very pretty when you were young,' he said, pointing to a photograph of me when I was six, on the beach at Malibu with my father.

'Oh, so you don't think I'm pretty now?' I said, pretending to be offended.

Anton blushed and said quickly, 'No, I do not – I mean, yes, I – ' He stopped and then gave me a sheepish grin. 'I'm sorry, my English is not good. I do not mean to be impolite. I am sorry.'

'That's okay,' I said, and smiled at him as graciously as I could.

Anton took a step towards me and then stopped as I backed away. 'I have come to apologise,' he said. 'I have come to say I am sorry.'

'Seems to me you're always apologising for something.' I was trying hard to sound cold and unforgiving but I don't think my act was very convincing.

Anton took another step forward and this time I didn't move away. He shrugged and gazed at me soulfully. 'I always have much to say sorry for,' he said. 'But I want to explain to you. I want to tell you why I am upset. And why I am rude. You will understand when I tell you.'

'Try me,' I said. He needn't think that he could get round me with those cow eyes. He needn't think that I'd fall for that corny South American charm. He needn't think –

'Please,' he said. 'Come up to the – how you say? – penthouse and take refreshment with me and I will explain.'

I was taken aback. This was an offer I couldn't refuse. Or could I? 'Who else will be there?' I said weakly.

'Carlos, of course, and Josefina. Josefina, she would like especially to meet you. She has prepared some special delicacies. Food of my country.'

I put up a final frail line of defence. 'I've got a History assignment. I really should – '

Anton laughed. He knew as well as I did that this excuse was too feeble for words. 'You prefer History to my company? Okay, if that is the way you want it.'

I was astonished by his arrogance. How dare he assume that I'd be willing to stop everything just for a chance to spend some time with him! Who did he think he was?

'My studies are very important to me,' I said icily. 'I need to get good grades.'

'Just ten minutes,' he smiled. 'Surely you can spare ten

minutes from your History?'

I wavered. Anton Velasco was a self-centred creep but it *would* be interesting to take a good look at the penthouse. And I wanted to find out more about him. There were so many questions –

'Hang on a minute,' I said. 'I'll just tell Flanagan where I'm going.'

Anton waited in the hall while I rushed to my room and ran a comb through my hair. Then I popped my head into the sitting room to tell the others I was going upstairs. I'm glad to say that they were suitably impressed.

I was impressed too when I saw the penthouse. It was enormous, though I didn't think much of the interior decoration. The flat looked as though it had been furnished in a great hurry with no thought given to matching styles and colours. The chairs and pictures and carpets were obviously expensive but nothing seemed to go together. And there was none of the private clutter that can be seen in even the tidiest homes. No photographs or magazines or letters or other personal touches. It was rather like being in an empty luxury hotel. Still, we didn't stay long in the huge gloomy rooms but went straight out to sit in the roof garden. The grass and flower beds were looking a little untidy, but the effect was still as astonishing as I remembered. It seemed very odd to be sitting in a garden chair on a lawn under a cherry tree, seven storeys above ground.

There was no sign of Carlos, or anyone else for that matter, but after a minute or two a plump dark-haired woman in a white apron bustled outside, carrying a laden tray which she deposited on a wrought-iron table. She said something to Anton in Spanish, and then grinned at me. She seemed to have several teeth missing.

'This is Josefina,' Anton said. 'She is the wife of Carlos and a very good cook. She has brought fruit juice for you, and tequeños, and other things.'

'I wasn't expecting such a feast!' I said. 'Thank you, Josefina. You are most kind.'

Josefina beamed again before going back inside. I was starving and so I headed straight for the food. The tequeños were delicious; they were fingers of cheese fried in a sort of thin dough. There were little meat turnovers, too, which Anton said were called empanadas, and sweet yellowish fruit called sapodillas which we ate with coconut ice cream.

'All Venezuelan food,' Anton said proudly. I noticed that he ate hardly anything but seemed content to watch me making a pig of myself.

'Did Carlos and Josefina come with you from Venezuela?' I asked.

'Yes. They work for my father at the hacienda in Merida. Then they come to London with me. Life is very dull for them here, I think.'

'And cold, too, I expect.' I poured myself a glass of fruit juice and then settled back in my chair. 'Do your parents live here, too?'

'No, just me and Carlos and Josefina,' Anton said. 'Sometimes my mother is here for a few days only. She travels a great deal. We have a flat in Paris also, and she likes that better. And Spain too. Once a month, perhaps, she is here.'

'And what about your father?'

'He is in Venezuela. He will come here for a visit, maybe. Who knows?'

There was a pause. I could hear the distant hum of traffic far below us. I was dying to know more about Anton but it seemed rude to ask any more questions. Then I remembered all the questions he had fired at *me* the day before. He hadn't been worried about hurting *my* feelings. So why should I be worried about his?

'But why are *you* living here?' I asked. 'All on your own.'

Anton grinned ruefully. 'It was decided I should have an English education,' he said.

'English education!' I gave a yelp of laughter. 'You should go to Eton or Grange Hill if you want an English education. You won't get it at Chalfont. It's a good school, all right, but it's not exactly *English*, is it?'

Anton looked puzzled. 'Isn't it?'

'Of course not. Oh, I know a few people are doing A-Levels but most of us take the International Baccalaureate course because it's recognised all over the world. Chalfont's an international school, really.'

Anton got up then and walked across the lawn towards the low wall that surrounded the terrace. I put down my glass and joined him. Together we looked out across the rooftops towards the zoo and the park. The Snowdon Aviary at the zoo looked like a couple of crumpled steel coathangers. Beyond it stretched the trees of Regent's Park.

'What an amazing view,' I said. 'You can see for miles.'

'Is very boring,' Anton said absently. 'Is nothing to see but grey buildings and green trees. Green, green, nothing

54

but green. There is no colour in this country.' He paused, and then went on, 'I have to tell you something. I will tell you the truth. You will understand then why – why I am sometimes strange in my behaviour.'

'Not strange,' I said. 'Just rude, that's all.'

He turned and grinned. 'I know. I am sorry for that.' Then he looked out again across the park. 'My father, he is very rich. Very rich and powerful man in Venezuela. From coffee.'

'Coffee? I thought coffee came from Brazil.'

Anton shot me an irritated glance. 'Not all of it,' he said frostily. Then he went on, 'We have big estates in the mountains. And house at Altamira also, near Caracas.' He turned and wandered back towards the chairs. 'But there is much danger from kidnappers in my country.'

'Kidnappers?'

'Yes. There are people who will kidnap children of rich parents and demand a ransom for their return. It is the same in every country. Sometimes they do not give the child back when money is paid. Sometimes –'

'That's dreadful!' I said.

'Yes, it is dreadful. Last year, our friend Lucia Fernandez was taken and they cut off her ear to send to her parents. She is seventeen years old.'

I was horrified. Instinctively, I reached out and touched his hand and he turned towards me. 'My parents are frightened this will happen to me,' he said huskily. 'That is why they send me away. They think I will be safe in London. Here, with Carlos to protect me.'

And suddenly I understood. I understood why Carlos followed Anton everywhere and drove him to and from

55

school. I saw now why Anton seemed so edgy and nervous. He was frightened. Frightened of being attacked, frightened of being kidnapped.

'And are you safe here?' I whispered.

He shrugged. 'Who knows? Safer perhaps than Venezuela. I do not know. But Carlos is a good man, a strong fighter. He is an Andino, from the mountains. I am safe with him, I think.' He looked at me anxiously. 'But please, you will not tell anyone about this? You will not tell anyone at Chalfont?'

I shook my head. 'Of course not.'

'It shall be our secret,' Anton said, and took my hand for a moment. Then he let it fall and wandered across the garden to the opposite side. He looked suddenly lost and alone, very different from the arrogant boy I had met for the first time on Monday. It's true, I thought. Money isn't everything. It can't buy you happiness. Or love. I suppose most of us were unhappy in one way or another. People thought we were so lucky, going to school at Chalfont. They envied our glamorous, exciting lives. And perhaps they were right. I was lucky, I know. Our flat may not have been as luxurious as Anton's penthouse but it was large and comfortable and we lived well. I had a generous allowance and extra money when I needed it. But I would have given it all up in exchange for parents who loved each other, for a home where we could all be together. And Anton? He had all the money in the world but he was lonely and afraid.

'Melanie! Come here!'

I looked up, startled. Anton had turned and was beckoning to me. I ran to join him at the wall. 'What is it?' I

56

said as I reached him.

He was staring now at the block of flats opposite, at Park Plaza. 'You were right,' he murmured. 'You were right yesterday, when you spoke of someone watching. Look!'

I looked across and down at the familiar windows. The woman was there at her usual place, peering up through the curtains, watching. Watching us. And then she ducked quickly away, as though she knew she had been seen.

'Who is she?' I said urgently. 'Why is she watching you?'

'I do not know.' Anton's face was pale, his eyes bright and anxious.

'Should you tell Carlos?'

Anton gave a sharp laugh. 'What should I tell him? A woman is looking out of her window. Where is the harm in that?'

'But – but there's something *wrong* about her. I can't explain it but I just *know* that –'

He gave me a sharp look. '*What* do you know?'

'Nothing for certain,' I said. 'I just feel that she means harm.'

'Harm? To me?'

I shrugged. 'I don't know. Who else?'

Anton was silent for a moment. 'I cannot tell Carlos unless we are sure. He would go over there and –' He stopped, and gave a wry smile. 'He would make things difficult, shall we say. And if the woman is innocent – well, there would be unpleasantness. No, we must be sure. We must make sure that the woman is a threat before we tell Carlos. Before we tell anyone.'

'But how are we going to find out?'

Anton took both my hands in his. 'We will just have to think of something, won't we? We will have to think of a way to find out who she is. That watcher in the window. But do not worry. We will do it. Together.'

CHAPTER SIX

I can't remember much about the rest of that week. I know that I spent a good deal of it in a daze, not knowing whether I was coming or going most of the time. I couldn't work out my feelings for Anton. One half of me was fascinated by him and his strange, lonely life, while the rest of me was annoyed by his arrogance and rudeness. I'd never met anyone quite like him before. Heaven knows there were plenty of crazy and exotic people at Chalfont, with backgrounds just as curious as his. Yet the way he looked, his life alone in that vast apartment, his constant fear of danger – all these things combined to surround him with an air of mystery. It was almost as if he'd strayed from another planet.

Sometimes I wasn't even sure if he'd been telling me the truth. His story about Venezuela and kidnappers seemed too far-fetched for words; perhaps he was having me on, making fun of me while pretending to be little boy lost. How could I be sure? Then I remembered our time together in the roof garden, and Josefina and her tequeños, and I knew it must be true. And I hadn't imagined his fear when he'd seen the watcher. But, despite all this, Anton remained a mystery. I didn't know whether to like him or loathe him. In the end, I decided not to do either for the time being but wait and see what happened next.

In one way, though, my life changed for the better. When I left Anton's apartment that Wednesday evening, he told me that from then on he'd give me a lift to Chalfont every morning in the Mercedes. And back again, if our classes ended at the same time.

'Is more sensible,' he pointed out. 'We both go to the school in the morning. We should travel together. It is decided.'

And so it was. I can't say that I objected to the arrangement. It meant an end to my mad morning dashes and to my angry waits at the bus stop with Tammy-Ann Ziegler. And Theo and Flanagan liked it, too. I now had time to sit and have breakfast with them, not that I was very good company first thing in the morning.

But, apart from our brief journeys in the limousine, Anton and I didn't spend much time together during the next couple of days. Abby asked me round to her place after school on Thursday, and then, on Friday evening, some family friends of Anton's whisked him off to a function at the Venezuelan Embassy. When we met, we didn't discuss the watcher at all but that wasn't surprising. We could hardly talk about her in the car, with Carlos listening. I wasn't sure how well he understood English but I guessed he could speak it better than he pretended. And there wasn't any opportunity at Chalfont, of course. I tried not to look out for the watcher any more; I wanted to forget all about her if I could. But, time and again, I would find myself drawn to my window and the view of Park Plaza. Sometimes there would be nothing to see, other than the tidy curtains of the flat opposite; at others, I would spot the woman looking out, watching, always watching.

I said nothing of all this to Abby. Apart from anything else, I'd promised Anton that I wouldn't tell a soul. Abby and I talked about Anton, of course, when I went home with her on Thursday evening. I suppose there would have been no harm in telling her that I'd been up to his apartment but something stopped me. For some reason that I couldn't explain, I wanted those moments with Anton to be private – for the time being, anyway. I didn't want anyone to know about Anton or the watcher until I was quite certain how I felt about them myself. All the same, I felt horribly guilty about my silence, especially as Abby spent most of our time together on Thursday giving me all the gory details of her relationship with Gary Goldman.

'I don't know,' she sighed at one point. 'Sometimes I don't know where I am with Gary. One day I'll be furious with him and decide that I never want to see him again, and the next he just has to look at me with those deep blue eyes of his and I'm all of a quiver. What would *you* do, Mel?'

'Me?' I gave a sharp, bitter laugh. 'You're asking *me* for advice about how to deal with a boy like Gary? You must be joking!'

'I'm not joking,' Abby said seriously. 'I think there's a lot of common sense lurking under that cool exterior of yours. Anyway, you knew Jordan pretty well and he was Gary's best friend.'

Jordan. I didn't know him at all well. I thought I did. I thought I knew everything about him. But I realised now that I had never known him at all. And funnily enough, I didn't care any more.

'Don't talk to me about – ' I began, and then Abby interrupted me.

'Now what's all this about you and Latin Lover Velasco?' she said. 'Come on, tell your Auntie Abby all. You've been seen emerging from his Merc with a smug expression on your face. What's going on, Mel?' She dug me in the ribs. 'You told *me* that he's a jerk and that you didn't want anything to do with him.'

'He *is* a jerk. I mean – er – he *isn't* but –' I could feel my face reddening.

Abby regarded me with amusement. 'She's blushing, the girl's blushing!' she crowed. 'It *must* be love!'

'Oh, shut up!' I snapped. 'He just happens to live in my block and so he gives me a lift to school in the morning, that's all.'

'A lift and what else?'

'What do you mean, what else? Nothing else.'

'Oh, yes? And do you really expect me to believe that?'

'Yes, you klutz!' I laughed and flung a cushion at her. 'Anyway, he's not interested in me. Not in that way.'

'What do you mean?' Abby asked.

'Well, just look at me,' I said. 'I'm not exactly Anton's type, am I?'

'And what exactly *is* his type?'

I wasn't altogether sure. 'Someone tall and dark and amusing and attractive and –'

'In other words,' Abby said gently, 'someone exactly like you.'

I laughed out loud. 'You must be joking!'

'No, I'm not,' she said. 'I'm serious. I just wish you'd stop running yourself down, that's all.'

I didn't know what to say at first. I was too embarrassed. Then I decided to change the subject. 'Anyway,' I said loudly, 'there's not much that *can* happen in the back seat of a Merc at half past eight in the morning. Not with his chauffeur watching,' I added quickly.

'Oh, so that's who he is? The mysterious man in black. He's just a driver. How boring.'

'Yes, how boring,' I said.

If only you knew, I thought. Oh, Abby, if only you knew.

It wasn't until Saturday morning that Anton mentioned the watcher again. I had just woken up and was thinking how marvellous it was to have two whole days in front of me with nothing to do, when the phone rang. Flanagan answered and then came padding down the passage to my door.

'Okay, I'm coming!' I yelled, and staggered blearily to the phone. Flanagan gave me a knowing smile before disappearing into her room. She was wearing a track suit and was looking rather red in the face, the result of her regular early morning run. Flanagan's a fitness freak; it comes from being Australian, I expect.

I picked up the receiver, and croaked, 'Hullo?'

I had been expecting to hear Abby's voice in reply and so I was taken aback to find instead that the caller was Anton. It was the first time I'd spoken to him on the phone; his voice sounded even sexier than it did face to face. If that were possible.

'Ah, good, it is you,' he said briskly. 'Today we will

solve the mystery of the woman at the window. I will meet you in ten minutes.'

'Hey, hang on!' I protested feebly. 'I've only just woken up. And anyway, what's the hurry? Another hour or so isn't going to make any difference.' Apart from anything else, I liked to take my time getting up on Saturdays. I enjoyed making the most of a free morning.

'Very well,' he said wearily. 'You tell me the time you are ready.'

'Ten o'clock,' I said firmly.

Anton sighed. 'Very well, if is what you want.'

'Is what I want,' I said, then, 'but what are you going to do about Carlos? We don't want him tagging along, do we?'

'I have already thought of that,' Anton said smugly. 'I am sending him to Harrods for some shopping. Bread. Milk. Things like that. When he has gone, I will leave the flat and meet you outside Park Plaza. At ten o'clock.'

'I'll be there,' I said. I wondered if Anton always bought his bread at Harrods.

'Do not be late,' he said sharply. 'Already we waste much time.'

I was about to say something rude in reply and then decided against it. But the sooner I showed Anton Velasco that I wasn't going to be bossed around the better. Maybe it would do him good to be kidnapped. It would certainly take him down a peg or two.

I grinned at the thought as I said, 'Goodbye, Anton,' and put down the receiver.

When I arrived outside Park Plaza later that morning, Anton was already waiting grumpily on the other side of the street.

'You are late,' he said accusingly when he saw me.

'Yes,' I said. I didn't see why I should make any excuses so I didn't. 'What do we do now?'

'We look,' Anton said. 'We look at the building and try to work out which is the apartment of the watcher.'

'That's easy,' I said. 'It's on the top floor. On the left-hand side.'

Anton looked at me pityingly. 'Looking from our building it is on left-hand side,' he explained. 'But from other side, *this* side, it is on right.'

Oh well, logic was never my strong point. I crossed the road to take a closer look at Park Plaza. It was six floors high and seemed to be constructed mainly of glass. It didn't look as solid or as welcoming as the block where Anton and I lived; in fact, it looked as though the entire building might collapse in the first strong wind. There was an elaborate garden at the front, with a lily pond and exotic large-leafed shrubs, and there seemed to be more plants in the spacious lobby.

There was a panel of bells and nameplates beside the main door, twelve of them altogether. I looked for the name Ziegler and found it next to the bell marked No. 4. That ruled out Tammy-Ann as the guilty party, anyway. Apartment four was on the first floor, not the fifth.

'The top apartments will be numbers eleven and twelve,' Anton said thoughtfully. 'But which is which, I wonder?' He peered at the names. 'Rogers is in eleven and Ans – I cannot say the name – '

'Anstruther,' I said.

'Anstruther in number twelve.'

'It must be Anstruther,' I said. 'Look, the odd numbered apartments are all on the left-hand side. So the top right-hand apartment will be number twelve.'

'So it is Miss Anstruther who is watching me,' Anton said. 'Who is this Miss Anstruther, I wonder?'

'That's what we must find out,' I said. 'But how?'

Anton was trying the glass entrance doors now but I guessed they would only open from the inside. Then he pressed a button marked 'Porter' and I hissed, 'What on earth are you doing?'

He gave me a warning glance, and I kept silent. After a moment, a door at the rear of the lobby opened and a red-faced man in an overall looked out. He saw us waiting, and came across and opened the doors.

'Yes?' he said crossly. 'What d'you want?'

'I am sorry to disturb you,' Anton said. 'Please help me. I want to see the old friend of my mother, Miss Ans –'

'Anstruther,' I prompted.

'Anstruther. I ring the bell but is no reply. Perhaps she is out or maybe the bell is broken. Can you tell me, please, if Miss Anstruther is here?'

The porter looked offended. 'I'll have you know that all the bells are in proper working order. In fact,' he went on angrily, 'all the electrics is in proper working order. As for your Miss Anstruther, I take it you mean *Mrs* Anstruther. Flat twelve is occupied by Mr and *Mrs* Anstruther.'

Anton gave a beaming smile and then slapped his forehead with the palm of his hand. 'Of course!' he cried. '*Mrs* Anstruther, yes. It is *Mrs* Anstruther who is dear friend of my mother. *That* is the lady I must see. She is in? I can see her?'

The porter was clearly not impressed by Anton's theatrical display of Latin charm. He stared at him stonily and said, 'That would be a little difficult, sir. Mr and Mrs Anstruther are in Italy. Seeing as how your mother is such a dear friend of Mrs Anstruther, I'm surprised she didn't tell you that the lady and her husband spend three months of the year at their home there.'

Oh dear. Now we're for it. I closed my eyes and waited for Anton's reply. His first ploy hadn't worked. What would he try next?

I didn't have to wait long. 'Of course I know they go to Italy,' he said indignantly. 'Have I not myself been to their lovely villa at Rapallo?'

I opened my eyes again in amazement. Anton was glaring scornfully at the porter as if he had just discovered a particularly unpleasant type of cockroach. 'Of course I know they go to Italy,' he repeated. 'But my mother, she told me they return in April.'

The porter was looking less stony now. 'No, sir,' he said, a little uneasily, I thought. 'I'm afraid you've been misinformed. My instructions are that they will not be returning until June. Besides, their tenant is still – '

'Tenant?' I said in surprise.

The cockroach looked at me with contempt for a moment and then turned back to Anton. 'Their tenant is still in residence,' he went on. 'As far as I'm aware, her lease expires at the end of May. And now if you'll excuse me – '

He started to turn away but stopped when Anton said, 'Tenant? What tenant?'

The cockroach was beginning to get annoyed now. 'Mr

and Mrs Anstruther have sub-let their flat for a few months, not that it's anything to do with – '

'Who is she?' I blurted out. 'What's her name?'

The cockroach stared at me in astonishment. 'I'm afraid that's no business of *yours*, young lady,' he said, and closed the heavy glass doors firmly in our faces.

Anton and I retreated to the other side of the street and began to walk slowly towards the park. After a while, I stopped and turned to him. He seemed to be deep in thought.

'So, what happens now?' I asked.

He smiled ruefully and shrugged. 'We must think,' he said. 'We must think *very* carefully.'

'We haven't got very far. All we know is that the woman watching you is a tenant of Mr and Mrs Anstruther. We can't ask them about her as they're in Italy. By the way,' I added, remembering, 'how do you know that their villa is in Rapallo?'

Anton grinned. 'I don't. I invented it. Very convincing, I think.'

'Brilliant,' I said. 'Pity it didn't get us anywhere. As I was saying, the porter is the only person who knows who the tenant is but *he* won't tell us. Hey, didn't he remind you of a cockroach?'

'The porter?' Anton murmured and then laughed. 'Yes, a cockroach. A big, fat cucuracha. Yes, you are right.'

'So? What do we do next?'

Anton turned and looked back at Park Plaza. I followed his gaze. Pale spring sunlight sparkled on the windows, and a red and white striped awning hung over one of the upper balconies. Then, as we watched, the front door opened and a woman came out. A grey-haired woman with glasses, wearing a green coat.

'Oh my God, look!' I breathed. 'Look who it is!'

'It is her!' Anton gasped. 'The woman in the window. Miss Anstruther.'

'Her name isn't Miss Anstruther,' I hissed. 'We don't know what her name is.'

Anton waved a dismissive hand. 'Does not matter. For me, her name is Miss Anstruther.'

I understood what he meant. Even though it wasn't her real name, it did give the mysterious watcher a sort of identity at last.

Miss Anstruther paused outside the building and then began to walk up the road, away from us.

'Did she see us?' I hissed.

'No,' said Anton. 'I'm sure she did not. Come on.' And he started to walk back the way we had come, in the direction that the woman had taken.

I gaped at him. 'Where – where are you going?'

He didn't stop. 'We must follow her. Come on, quickly. We must not lose her.'

I burst out laughing as I ran to catch him up. It was like something from a bad TV movie. Anton surely didn't expect us to –

'If we follow her, we may discover useful information,' Anton said curtly. 'It is worth a try.' He stopped suddenly and turned to me. 'Have you any better ideas?'

'No.'

'Good.' He set off again at a brisk pace. 'We shall see what we shall see.'

We followed the green coat round the corner into St

John's Wood Terrace and then up into Acacia Road. The woman stopped occasionally to peer into shop windows, forcing us to dive for cover behind trees or parked cars. I felt ridiculous. We were sixteen years old, not six. We were too old to be playing games.

Anton looked cross when I complained to him. 'She must not see us,' he said. 'If she knows we are following, then we will discover nothing. And we are not playing games. If this Miss Anstruther is a danger to me, then I must know.' When I started to protest, he added, 'You do not have to come. You can go home, if you want. I will follow her alone.'

I didn't want to follow Miss Anstruther. But I didn't want to go home, either. I wanted to stay with Anton, and if that meant playing cops and robbers – well, that was the price I'd have to pay.

'Okay, you win,' I muttered, and then, 'look, she's on the move again.'

We followed the woman along Acacia Road as far as the tube station. She paused outside to buy a newspaper and then joined the queue at the ticket window. We waited until two or three other people had fallen in behind her and then we joined the queue ourselves.

Anton was looking worried for the first time that day. 'I have never been on underground,' he explained. 'Here is money. Please, you get tickets.'

I stared at him in surprise. Never been on the underground? And then I remembered Carlos and the Mercedes. Of course. Anton wouldn't be allowed to travel about on his own.

He nudged me. 'Look, she is buying ticket now.'

We were too far away from Miss Anstruther to hear what she said at the ticket window but I bought two singles to Embankment when our turn came. If she travelled further on, we would just have to pay extra at the other end.

By the time we reached the escalator, Miss Anstruther was already near the bottom. I ran down the staircase after her while Anton followed more timidly behind. He caught up with me at the bottom, and we ran together towards the southbound platform. We couldn't see the woman at first, and for a moment I thought she might be waiting on the northbound side. I hadn't heard a train come in so it was unlikely that she was already on her way. Then Anton caught sight of the green coat at the far end of the platform, and we sidled towards her until we had a clear view. She was staring at a large advertisement for foreign language lessons, and didn't look in our direction at all.

We didn't sit down in the train when it came but stood by the doors so that we could peer out at each station to see if Miss Anstruther got off. Even so, we nearly lost her. So many people got out at Charing Cross that I wasn't able to see if she had left the train or not. It was Anton who spotted the green coat passing down the platform and gave me a warning push. We rushed from the carriage just as the doors were closing, and then had to struggle through the crowds until we had the woman clearly in sight once more.

It wasn't as easy to follow Miss Anstruther now. There were many more people in the tube station and, when we reached ground level, the crowds and traffic increased as we approached Trafalgar Square. Anton was so astonished

71

by the sight of Nelson's Column that he was almost knocked down by a taxi as we crossed the Strand. All the same, we managed to keep the green coat in sight past the South African Embassy and St Martin's-in-the-Fields. Then, as we approached the Edith Cavell statue, Miss Anstruther crossed the road and went into the National Portrait Gallery.

We had to wait ages for a gap in the traffic before we could follow the woman into the gallery and so there was no sign of her when we came to a breathless halt in the entrance hall.

'What shall we do?' I asked Anton.

He looked round wildly. Ahead of us were staircases leading up and down, and to the left a door led into the gallery souvenir shop.

'You look there,' he said, pointing at the shop, 'and downstairs. I will go up to the floor above. We will meet back here.' And he headed briskly for the staircase.

'But what are we looking –' I began, and then stopped. Anton was now out of sight. I'd no idea what I was supposed to do if I did find Miss Anstruther. Keep watching her, I supposed. But why? I shrugged, and turned left into the shop.

Miss Anstruther wasn't there among the postcards and books, though it took me some time to make sure. The room was crowded with schoolgirls in hideous purple blazers, and with American tourists buying postcards of kings and queens. There was nothing much to be seen downstairs, certainly not Miss Anstruther, and so I made my way back to the entrance hall. What should I do now? I decided to explore further, and I made for the staircase.

I'd never been in the National Portrait Gallery before and so I was surprised to discover that it wasn't just a collection of boring old pictures of kings. In fact, I was so fascinated by the contemporary section, which had sculptures and photographs and videos of pop stars and politicians as well as paintings, that I completely forgot what I was supposed to be doing there. As soon as I remembered, I galloped back downstairs to find Anton.

He was sitting in the entrance hall when I arrived, looking pale and puzzled.

'Sorry I'm late,' I said. 'I couldn't find her anywhere. Did you?'

Anton nodded. 'Yes, I saw her.' He stared at the floor, apparently lost in thought.

'Well?' I asked impatiently. 'What happened? Where is she now?'

Anton shrugged. 'I do not know where she is now. I lost her. After –'

'After what?'

He turned to me. 'I followed her upstairs. She look at pictures here and there, and then she went up more stairs and looked for a long time at a big picture of your Princess of Scotland.'

'Princess of Scotland?' What on earth was he talking about?

Anton waved an impatient hand. 'Yes, Princess of Scotland. Your Diana.'

Light dawned. 'She's not my Diana,' I said irritably. 'And she's Princess of Wales, not Scotland.'

Anton raised his eyes heavenwards with exasperation. 'Scotland, Wales, what does it matter? She look at the picture for a long time, as if she is waiting for somebody. And then – and then a man comes up and talks to her.'

'A man?'

'Yes, a man. A man in a suit, with black curly hair.'

'And then what happened?'

'They move away to the side of the room and talk. Then he gives her an envelope and she puts it in her handbag.'

'An envelope? What was in it? Money?'

Anton gave me a scowl. 'Don't be stupid. How do I know what is in it?'

'Okay, okay, don't bite my head off. What happened next?'

'Then they talk some more and the man goes away. Downstairs. Miss Anst – er –'

'Anstruther.'

'Yes, Miss Anstruther, she waits for a moment and then goes down the stairs too.'

'And where is she now?'

Anton looked at me unhappily. 'I do not know. She was coming straight towards me and so I went into another room so that she would not see me. When I came out again, she was gone. I have lost her.'

I felt a surge of relief at this news. I was in no mood for following Miss Anstruther round London for the rest of the day. 'Can't be helped,' I said cheerfully.

'As you say, it can't be helped,' Anton said mournfully. 'But the man – that man –'

'What about him?'

Anton turned to me, a puzzled frown on his face. 'I have seen him before,' he said slowly. 'I am sure I have seen him before. Somewhere. I know the face. I *know* it.'

'Who is it?' I asked eagerly.

Anton smiled ruefully and shrugged. 'I do not know. I cannot remember. I cannot remember who it is.'

'Someone from Venezuela?'

'Perhaps. And if it is someone from Venezuela, why is he here? What does he want with that woman who watches me? What are they planning? Is it to harm me? Is it?'

Anton stared at me, his eyes wide with alarm. He suddenly looked about four years old and I resisted an urge to fling my arms around him. Instead I said gently, 'I don't know, Anton. I don't know. But don't worry. We'll tell the police if we have to. And Carlos is there to help you.' I paused, and added, 'And me, too.'

Anton gave me a sad smile and took my hand. 'Yes, I am lucky,' he whispered. 'I have Carlos. And you too, Melanie.'

'Call me Mel,' I said huskily. 'All my friends do.'

'Mel,' he whispered. 'I am glad to be your friend, Mel.' Then he stood up. 'Now we must go back to the flat. Carlos will be very angry that I have gone.'

'Do we have to go back?' I asked, as I followed him out of the gallery. 'It's such a nice day. We could – oh, I don't know –'

Anton stopped on the pavement outside and turned to look at me, his face lit up by a broad, mischievous grin. 'You are right,' he said. 'We need not go back yet. I will phone and tell Carlos that I am okay, that *you* are protecting me. And then,' he went on, stretching his arms wide and almost braining a passing Japanese tourist in the process, 'and then I want to see London. All of London! You will show it to me, Mel. I have been already two weeks in London and I have seen only Harrods and the Embassy of Venezuela.'

I laughed out loud and took his hand, and we ran across the road to the Post Office near St Martin's-in-the-Fields to telephone Carlos and Flanagan to say we wouldn't be home. Then we walked down to Trafalgar Square to look at Nelson's Column and the pigeons. The sun was shining and suddenly summer didn't seem too far away. For an hour or two we could forget all about Miss Anstruther and kidnappers and the man in the gallery.

There are some days that linger in the memory for years afterwards, days that stay special forever. That day was one of them. Anton wanted to see the sights of London and I was only too glad to keep him company. From Trafalgar Square, we walked under Admiralty Arch and down the Mall to Buckingham Palace, where we stared through the railings, hoping for a glimpse of the Princess of Scotland. But she didn't seem to be at home and so we wandered into St James's Park instead and sat in the sun and watched the ducks on the lake for a while. Then we began to feel hungry and so we took a taxi to Covent Garden and bought burgers and doughnuts to eat in the shady garden behind St Paul's Church. A juggler was rehearsing his act on the grass, and we sat and watched him as we shared our lunch with the sparrows. Then we wandered back across the piazza and in and out of the shops and stalls that filled the old market. We stopped to eat ice cream and to listen to a jazz band that was entertaining the crowds and then we walked on again, hand in hand, this time towards Charing Cross Road where Anton bought a very large book about parrots in a second-hand book-shop. When we reached Tottenham Court Road tube station he said, 'And now we *must* go home,' but I said, 'No, not yet,' and we went instead to the cinema across the road and saw the new Woody Allen movie that Tammy-Ann Ziegler had been talking about on Monday. We sat near the back and ate popcorn. And then, when the movie began, Anton put his arm around me and I rested my head on his shoulder. His skin smelt faintly of soap, cool and tangy. And after that, we *did* go home but by bus this time, a bright red 113. We got off by the mosque and walked the rest of the way as slowly as possible because we didn't want the day to end.

'What happens now?' I said, as we came in sight of our building at last.

'What do you mean?'

'Miss Anstruther. What do we do now? We haven't got much further, have we? We haven't found out who she is.'

Old Cocky Nose peered out at us from his cubby-hole as we walked into the lobby, and I gave him a wave.

Anton pressed the button for the elevator. 'We must have evidence before we can accuse her,' he said thoughtfully.

'But how can we get it?'

The elevator doors opened and we stepped inside. I pressed the button for my floor and the doors closed gently behind us.

'There is only one way,' Anton said. 'We must get inside her apartment.'

I stared at him, aghast. 'Get inside her apartment? But how on earth –'

'Do shut up, Mel,' Anton said quietly. 'You talk too

much.'

And then he tilted my chin and traced my lips with his finger, and then he kissed me, very slowly.

As I said, there are some days that stay special for ever.

CHAPTER SEVEN

'Perhaps we should just tell someone all about it,' I said. 'The police, or someone.'

'Tell them what?' said Anton. 'Please sir, a woman is watching me from her window? Please sir, I follow that woman to a picture gallery and she talked to a man there? Please, Mr Policeman, sir, put the nasty lady in prison for me?'

'Well, perhaps not,' I said, and giggled. I'm not usually given to giggling – I leave that sort of thing to people like Tammy-Ann Ziegler – but I was feeling a bit hysterical that Sunday afternoon. I had a nasty suspicion that I was falling in love and I wasn't sure that I liked what was happening. But just because Anton had kissed me, very nicely, in the lift didn't mean anything at all. It didn't mean that he felt the same way about me as I did about him. Or did it? He'd phoned me twice yesterday evening but that didn't mean anything either. He'd known I'd be anxious to hear that he'd made it back to the penthouse safely. He'd realised that I wanted to know how angry Carlos had been. Very angry, apparently. Still, phone calls don't mean much. But surely that kiss did? And surely his suggestion that we spend Sunday afternoon together meant something too, if only that he liked my company.?

I sneaked a quick glance at him. He was lying on his

back on the grass, gazing up at the sky. We'd met after lunch and walked round Regent's Park for a while before staggering to the top of Primrose Hill to look at the view. Carlos had followed us every step of the way. He was sitting a few yards away from us now, looking thoroughly bad-tempered and out of place. It would have helped if he'd taken off his black raincoat at least.

I tickled Anton's nose with a piece of grass, and he grabbed my hand and held it. 'We cannot tell the police yet,' he said drowsily. 'We cannot tell anyone until we have proof.'

'We've got to do something,' I said.

'We will do as I said. We will get into the apartment of that woman.'

'But *how?*'

Anton waved his free hand dismissively. 'I will think of something.'

'*We* will, you mean.'

'You, me, it is the same.' He closed his eyes.

I bent down to kiss the end of his nose and then I caught sight of Carlos glaring at me and changed my mind. I now knew what it must have been like to have a chaperone watching one's every move.

I sat up and stared at the view. At the bottom of the hill lay the zoo, and I could see the angular aviary and the bronze-green roofs of the elephant house above the trees. Beyond, London stretched to the horizon like a grey stone sea. It was a bright, clear day and I could see the tower of Big Ben in the distance. To the left, the dome of St Paul's was dwarfed by the skyscrapers of the City.

'Is interesting view,' said a voice by my side. Anton was

sitting up again. Bits of grass were clinging to his hair and I brushed them gently away. 'London is so grey,' he went on sorrowfully. 'And green. Grey and green.' He turned to me. 'You must come with me to Venezuela,' he said excitedly, 'then you will see beauty. You will not believe the trees, the colour in the streets. Jacaranda, bougainvillea, flame-of-the-forest, all so beautiful . . .' His voice faded and he stared into the distance. I wondered what he was seeing. Not London, that was certain. His home, perhaps. His family.

'Have you got any brothers and sisters?' I asked. I seemed to know so little about him.

'No. There is only me. Perhaps that is why my father is so frightened for me. If I am lost, there is no one else.'

I squeezed his hand and looked quickly away. I couldn't bear the thought of anything happening to Anton. Not now. Not ever.

'We must decide,' I said briskly. 'We must decide how to get into the flat. We don't have a key so –'

'So we break the door down.'

I gave him a push. 'Oh, very clever. I can just see us doing *that*. No, we have to get in some other way.'

'The only other way is with a key,' Anton said.

'I know. And we also have to find a way into the building itself. The cucuracha isn't going to let us in. Not after yesterday.'

'I hadn't thought of that. It seems that you are not as stupid as you look.'

I tried to hit him then but he caught hold of my wrist and we wrestled enjoyably for a moment or two before collapsing on the grass once again.

'No,' Anton said at last. 'No, it will be difficult to get inside. What we need is help. Help from someone on the inside. Someone who lives there.'

'Yes,' I murmured. 'Someone who lives there. But who?'

In my mind's eye I could see the entrance to Park Plaza, and the panel of bells and nameplates . . .

I sat up with a jerk. 'Tammy-Ann Ziegler!' I yelped.

Anton sat up too, and stared at me in alarm. 'What's the matter?'

'Of course!' I said. 'Tammy-Ann Ziegler lives at number four.' I turned excitedly to him. '*You* know Tammy-Ann. The blonde who –'

'Ah, yes.' He grinned. 'The one with the voice. I know her, yes. She has been very friendly to me at Chalfont.'

I bet she has, I thought grimly. You could always rely on Tammy-Ann to be friendly to any new boy in town. Especially one as gorgeous as Anton.

'She lives in Park Plaza,' I explained. '*She* can let us in.'

Anton looked doubtful. 'But we would have to tell her everything,' he said slowly. 'And I'm not sure if she can be trusted. How can we know she will not tell others?'

'We don't need to tell her *anything* to start with,' I said. 'I can go and see her and have a quick look round the building at the same time. Spy out the land and all that.'

'But won't she be surprised to see you?' Anton asked. 'You are not great friends, I think. She will be suspicious.'

I hadn't thought of that. Tammy-Ann would most certainly be suspicious if I suddenly became terribly friendly with her.

'Leave it to me,' I said. 'I'll think of something.'

It took me the rest of that day and a good part of the evening to think of something. After all, it's not easy to come up with a convincing reason to be friendly with someone you've ignored for years. Tammy-Ann and I had nothing in common, apart from the fact that we both went to Chalfont. Mind you, I didn't know her well enough to be entirely sure about that. Maybe she shared my passion for chocolate chip ice cream and tacos. Maybe she hated apricots and Clint Eastwood as much as I did. I'd no way of telling. Perhaps we'd find we had so much in common that we'd be life-long friends. Then I remembered her voice and decided that there wasn't much chance of that.

I told Anton not to wait for me after school on Monday, as I wanted to travel home with Tammy-Ann Ziegler. My last class that day was French, which Tammy-Ann took too, and I planned to get into conversation with her after school. But it wasn't as easy as that. Abby grabbed my arm as I made for the door and asked me to have a soda with her at Gino's on the way home. I shook my head and muttered something about catching up on my History and then galloped after Tammy-Ann, leaving Abby puzzled and angry behind me. I'd explain everything to her tomorrow, I decided. I felt mean not telling her about Anton and Miss Anstruther and my sudden interest in Tammy-Ann Ziegler, but I just couldn't. Not yet, anyway.

Tammy-Ann looked at me in surprise when I joined her at the bus stop, though she wasn't as surprised as her best friend, Elaine Picillo, the biggest mooch in our year. Elaine gawped at me in silence as I chatted to Tammy-Ann about the kind of things that interested her: her latest boyfriend, Tara Lenkowsky's new hairstyle, what it would be like being married to Prince Edward, and whether Jim Curtis was gay. Then Elaine's bus came, and I had Tammy-Ann to myself at last.

I turned to her and lowered my voice confidentially. 'Look, Tammy-Ann, I'd value your advice about something.'

Her eyes widened in astonishment. 'Sure, Melanie,' she screeched. 'If I can, but – '

'You see, you've got so much more – more *experience* of boys than I have,' I went on. 'You'll know exactly what I should do.'

Tammy-Ann clearly didn't know whether to look pleased, superior or suspicious but she settled in the end for the latter. 'What do you mean by *experience*?'

'Don't get me wrong,' I said quickly. 'You just know how to *handle* boys better than I do . . .'

Tammy-Ann looked even more suspicious than before. 'What exactly do you mean by *handle*?'

'Tammy-Ann, *please*.' I was trying hard not to laugh out loud. Not for the first time, I wished that I had Abby's talent for acting. She'd really have made the most of this situation. 'I need your help. I do, honestly.'

Our bus came then and we scrambled inside. I sat down beside Tammy-Ann and whispered, 'You remember Jordan Macdonald, don't you? Of course you do. Well, you know – how much we cared for each other?'

Tammy-Ann nodded vigorously. At last we were on the same wavelength.

'Well,' I went on, 'I've had a letter from him and I don't know what to do about it. You see, Anton Velasco and I – '
I turned round dramatically to make sure no one was

listening. 'Well, Anton and I are seeing each other. And I don't know what to do about Jordan.'

It was all lies, of course. I knew exactly what to do about Jordan. Forget all about him. But Tammy-Ann didn't know that. And this was just the sort of situation she enjoyed.

'So I wondered if I could talk to you about it,' I said. 'Maybe we could go to your place? It's so noisy at our house with my brother and everything . . .' I looked at Tammy-Ann as appealingly as I could.

She hesitated for a moment or two, then, 'Sure, Mel,' she said. 'I'll be glad to help. Come and have a coke.'

I sat back and smiled to myself. Success at last!

It felt strange to walk into the lobby of Park Plaza once again and to know that, this time, I had every right to be there. There was no sign of the cockroach; instead a much younger man with a shock of fair hair was sitting the porter's office. Tammy-Ann gave him a wave as we passed.

'Who's that?' I hissed, as we waited for the elevator.

She looked at me in surprise. 'The doorman, of course. Well, one of them. We have two. The other one's an old grouch.'

I didn't tell her that I already knew that. Instead I said, 'Really?'

'Yeah,' Tammy-Ann screeched. 'But George is real cute. I like him.'

So there were two porters at Park Plaza, the cockroach and George. I tucked the information into my memory.

Much to my surprise, I quite enjoyed the next hour or so at Tammy-Ann's. The apartment was comfortable and welcoming and so was Tammy-Ann's plump mother who made sure we had all we needed to eat and drink before leaving us alone in Tammy-Ann's room. Her father was an executive in the London office of an American electronics company – at least, I think that's what Tammy-Ann said – but she and her parents didn't like England much and were living only for the day when they could return to Fort Wayne, Indiana. Wild horses couldn't have dragged me anywhere *near* Fort Wayne, Indiana, but I thought it polite not to say so. Instead, I told Tammy-Ann all about Jordan and a lot about Anton, much more than I'd intended. And then she told me all about Drain and how wonderful he was. After that, we had some more coke and angel food cake and parted the best of friends. Oddly enough, I felt clearer now about my feelings for Jordan and for Anton. Talking about them had helped. In fact, it was only when I was saying goodbye to Tammy-Ann that I remembered the real purpose of my visit. Miss Ans-truther.

Tammy-Ann saw me to the elevator so I had to press the button for the ground floor and pretend that I was leaving. But as soon as the lift reached the lobby, I pressed the top button and sailed upwards again, hoping that George hadn't noticed my abrupt arrival and departure. I don't know what I hoped to achieve by going to the top floor, but I felt I had to do *something*.

When the elevator doors opened again, I stayed where I was for a moment, uncertain what to do next. Then I stepped cautiously out of the lift. Facing me was a large window, which looked out over the street to the block of flats opposite. There was a sofa beneath the window, flanked by potted plants. To the left was the door to apartment twelve and, across the hall, was an identical door to apartment eleven. And that was all.

I stared at the door to apartment twelve. There it was. There was the door to the apartment where Miss Anstruther lived. Was she in there now, peering through the curtains, watching? It was strange to think that she might be on the other side of that plain wooden door.

And then, as I watched, the door opened. It was like a nightmare. I tried to run but I couldn't; my legs seemed as heavy as lead. I could only stand where I was, staring in horror, as the door opened slowly and a woman came out. A grey-haired woman in glasses, wearing a green coat.

Miss Anstruther.

CHAPTER EIGHT

I don't know which of us was the more surprised. Miss Anstruther and I stared at each other for what seemed hours but must have been only a couple of seconds. I could tell that she knew who I was and that she knew I'd recognised her. Her eyes were pale and cold behind her glasses, and her mouth was pinched and angry. She took a step towards me and I backed away towards the door of number eleven.

My mind raced frantically in search of something to say, something to break the threatening silence. But she was the one who spoke first.

'Looking for someone?' Her voice was harsh, with a slight accent that I couldn't quite place.

I gaped at her in desperation and then I suddenly remembered the door behind me, the door of the other apartment. An old couple lived there, the people with all the cats. What were they called? I dredged my memory for the name I'd seen by the bell downstairs. Roberts? Robins? Rogers? That was it, Rogers.

'I'm looking for Mr and Mrs Rogers,' I said. My voice sounded strangely shrill. 'I'm from the Cats' Protection League,' I went on. I can't imagine what made me say that but I always gabble when I'm nervous. I just say the first thing that comes into my head. 'I'm – I'm recruiting new members and Mr and Mrs Rogers have got cats and so I thought – '

'Well, then.' Miss Anstruther gave a thin, acid smile. 'You've come to the right place. That's their door behind you.'

I turned. 'Oh, yes. Of course. Thank you.' I rang the bell, praying that Mr and Mrs Rogers would be out. Miss Anstruther didn't move. I could feel her cold eyes boring into my back as I rang the bell again.

Then I heard someone coming to the door and my heart sank. It opened, and an elderly lady in a pink cardigan peered up at me.

'Mrs Rogers?' I said. 'I'm from the Cats' Protection League and I was wondering if you've ever considered – ' I rattled on about the benefits of the League and how important it was to protect cats and care for them properly. I thought I sounded pretty convincing for someone who comes up in a rash if a cat so much as looks at her.

There was a slight movement behind me, and I turned. Miss Anstruther had disappeared. I guessed that she'd gone back inside the flat and that she was standing by the door, listening. I turned back to the old lady and prepared to sing the praises of cats once again but she raised a pale hand to stop me.

'I don't quite understand, dear,' she said. 'We *are* members of the League. We have been for years.' She gave me a sweet, patient smile, and I grinned back.

'I'm sorry,' I said. 'Our records must be wrong. I'm sure they told me – '

'We pay our subscription regularly,' Mrs Rogers said, and then, 'I didn't know they sent – '

'Well, I'm sorry to have bothered you,' I said quickly, and backed away towards the lift. 'I'll make sure that head office is informed.'

Mrs Rogers smiled again, and then closed her door. I stood where I was for a moment, weak with relief. Then I dashed for the elevator and pressed the button. It seemed to take ages to arrive but at last it did and I leaped inside. Just before the doors closed, I saw Miss Anstruther's door open once more. She stepped out on to the landing and stood and watched me with her pale cold eyes until I disappeared from view.

By the time I got back to our apartment, I was trembling like a leaf. I'd now met the enemy face to face and I knew for certain that Miss Anstruther was not just an innocent Peeping Tom. I couldn't push the memory of those piercing eyes out of my mind and so I phoned Anton and asked him to come down.

It was a pleasant sunny evening but we didn't go out on the balcony. I wanted to stay as far away from those prying eyes as I could and so we went into my room, which looked out over the street on the other side of the building. Then I told Anton everything that had happened.

When I had finished, he came and sat beside me on the bed and took my hand in his. 'You are very brave, I think,' he said softly.

'Oh, nonsense,' I said, and stood up and crossed to the window. I felt restless and unsettled. 'I didn't do anything special. But that woman *is* a danger to you. I'm sure of it now. We've got to do something, Anton.'

He nodded. 'But we still have no proof. We *must* get into the flat. Always it comes back to that. There will be evidence in the flat, I know it. We must get inside.' He got up and put his arms around me. He hugged me tightly to him and I felt suddenly safe and secure.

'We'll just have to break in,' I said.

'Did the door have a Yale lock?'

I tried to remember. 'I think so. Why?'

'Perhaps we can get inside without much difficulty. I have read of using a credit card to open such locks.'

I looked up at his serious face and laughed out loud. 'You're joking!'

He shook his head. 'I am not joking. We must try it. We must try everything.'

I remembered my earlier encounter with Miss Anstruther and shivered. 'But we'll have to be sure she's out,' I said. 'There's no point in breaking into the flat if she's there.'

Anton frowned. 'I know that. I am not stupid. We must have a watcher of our own in Park Plaza. Someone who will tell us when Miss Anstruther goes out. Then we will get inside without her knowing.'

'But who?' I said petulantly. 'I hope you don't expect *me* to sit outside all day waiting for her to come out.'

'Of course not,' Anton said. 'We will ask someone else to keep watch. Someone who lives there already.'

I knew exactly who he meant. 'Tammy-Ann Ziegler, I suppose,' I said dully.

Anton gave me a broad, mocking grin. 'But of course,' he said. 'Who else?'

'We'll have to tell her everything.'

'I know.'

'And she won't believe a word of it. She won't be any

help at all.'

Anton shrugged. 'That is a chance we'll just have to take.'

I missed Tammy-Ann at the bus stop next morning and, at lunchtime, she disappeared in the direction of the High Street with Elaine Picillo before I had chance to speak to her. I was just about to follow them when I heard a shout behind me and I turned round and saw Abby waving frantically. I grinned and walked back to join her.

'Hi, stranger,' she said. 'I haven't seen you for days. Not to talk to, anyway.'

'I know,' I said guiltily.

'I bet you've been seeing Anton, though,' she went on. 'And Tammy-Ann Ziegler too, by the looks of it.' She stared at me curiously. 'Why are you and she such buddies all of a sudden? You told me you can't stand her.'

'I *can't* stand her,' I said. 'I mean, I can, but – '

'Oh, forget it,' Abby said frostily. 'It's nothing to do with me anyway. Listen, let's meet up tonight and have a – '

'I can't,' I said, wriggling with embarrassment. 'I'm sorry, Abby, I can't. I've something else on. I'm really sorry.'

Her face froze. She stared at me for a moment and then said, 'Okay. I get the picture.'

'No, you don't, Abby,' I said. 'I'm sure you don't. I'll tell you all about it soon, I promise, but – '

'Tell me now.' Her voice was as cold as her gaze.

'I can't. I promised – I can't, I'm sorry.' Then, as she turned away, 'But I will soon. I mean it. I'll tell you all about it soon.'

Abby shrugged and began to walk back to the school. Then she stopped suddenly and turned back to me. 'Oh, by the way, congratulations,' she said.

'Congratulations? What for?'

'You've got a part in *Our Town*. Just a walk-on but it's better than nothing. Maggie Farrell's put the cast list on the board. Your friend Tammy-Ann's got a part too, much to everyone's amazement. Still, she'll be playing an old gossip so her voice won't matter all that much.'

'And what about you?'

She gave a broad grin. 'I'm playing Emily,' she said. 'Believe it or not.'

'Oh, Abby, I *am* pleased,' I said and rushed over to give her a hug. 'I *knew* you'd get it. I knew it.'

'Did you? Did you really?' Then, when I nodded, she went on, 'Well, see you around, Mel. When you're ready.'

I nodded, and watched her as she crossed the lawn to the library. For a brief moment, I wondered whether to run after her and tell her all about Miss Anstruther and Anton. I could trust Abby, she was my friend. She wouldn't tell anyone else. Then I remembered Anton's dark imploring eyes and my promise to him. No, the only person we could tell was Tammy-Ann Ziegler. Because we needed her help.

I met up with her at last at the bus stop after school. She was with Elaine Picillo as usual and so I had to wait until Elaine had caught her bus before I could invite Tammy-Ann over to my place.

'I had such a lovely visit at your home,' I told her, 'and so it's only fair that you should come over to mine today.' I could see that she was uncertain and so I added slyly,

'Anton's going to be there.'

That clinched it. 'Why, thank you, Melanie,' she beamed. 'I'll be happy to.'

We talked about the play on the way home. Tammy-Ann was thrilled to have a part in *Our Town* and it wasn't long before the whole bus knew about it. She was playing Mrs Soames and I had to admit that Tammy-Ann would be ideal for the part. There's a lovely scene at the end of Act Two when Mrs Soames's chatter drowns out the minister's words at Emily's wedding. Tammy-Ann's screech would be just right for the character.

As soon as we arrived at the apartment, Tammy-Ann phoned her mother to tell her where she was and then I phoned Anton. He suggested that the two of us go up to the penthouse, an idea that filled Tammy-Ann with great excitement. I had to hand it to Anton – he certainly knew how to impress people. And he couldn't have thought of a better way of getting Tammy-Ann to eat out of his hand.

It wasn't until we had been on a conducted tour of the penthouse and enjoyed fruit juice and some of Josefina's tequeños that Anton raised the subject of Miss Anstruther. It was hard to tell whether Tammy-Ann believed the story or not but she listened wide-eyed and nodded eagerly when Anton asked her if she'd be willing to help us find a way into Miss Anstruther's apartment.

'Why not use a key?' she suggested. 'That's the easiest way, surely.'

We stared at her. 'A key?' Anton said at last. 'But where do we get a key?'

'From the porters, of course. They must have a pass key or duplicates or something. They must be able to get into the apartments in an emergency.'

Anton and I looked at each other. This was a possibility we hadn't considered.

'But how would we get it?' I asked.

Tammy waved a hand airily. 'Oh, I could manage that, I guess. I'll ask George. He'll do anything –'

'No,' Anton said firmly. 'We must not involve anyone else. And anyway, he will not give you the key, even if he has one.'

Tammy-Ann shrugged. 'Okay, if that's the way you want it. It was just a suggestion.'

'And a very good one, too,' Anton said huskily.

I gave him a sharp look. It seemed to me that he was laying on the sex-appeal a bit too generously for my liking. I didn't want Tammy-Ann to get any wrong ideas.

'We need you to be a look-out, Tammy-Ann,' I said loudly. 'We need you to tell us when Miss Anstruther goes out. Then, when you give us the signal –'

'What signal?'

'You will ring on the telephone to Mel's flat,' Anton said.

'Yes,' I said. 'Then when you ring through, we'll come over to Park Plaza and you'll let us into the building. Then we can take a good look at the apartment door and the lock without being disturbed.'

'What if she comes back before you've finished?' Tammy-Ann wanted to know.

'Give two rings on Miss Anstruther's phone. We should be able to hear it outside the door. Then we can nip down the stairs before she comes up in the lift.'

'But I don't know the number,' she protested. 'And we

don't know the woman's real name.'

'We don't *need* to know her real name,' I said witheringly. 'It'll be in the phone book under Anstruther.'

Tammy-Ann looked doubtful. 'I'm not sure –'

'It's all quite straightforward,' I said. 'You don't even need to move out of your apartment, except to let us into the building. You just need to keep watch on your balcony to see if she comes back.'

'*And* to see when she goes out,' Tammy-Ann said. 'I guess I'll be *living* out there from now on.' Then she had a sudden thought. 'When are we going to do all this, anyway?'

'It must be soon,' Anton said. 'The woman will be on her guard now. She knows that we are suspicious of her. So we must act quickly.'

'Before *she* does,' I put in.

'Yes,' Anton said. 'So you see, Tammy-Ann, we are depending on you. Your help is most important.' He lowered his voice. 'It is a matter of life and death. So it is most important you tell no one else. No one at all.'

'But I can tell Dane, can't I?'

'No,' I said firmly. 'You must tell no one. Not even Dr – Dane.'

Anton gave her one of his sultriest smiles. 'Mel is right, Tammy-Ann. No one must know. Not even Dr –'

'Dane,' I said quickly.

Tammy-Ann wavered. She looked at Anton, then at me, and then again at Anton. He gazed at her imploringly with his deep, dark eyes.

'Okay,' she said. 'I'll do it. I think you're both crazy but I'll do it.'

CHAPTER NINE

I didn't share Anton's confidence in Tammy-Ann's ability to help us. I knew that he put my doubts down to jealousy but that was just stupid. After all, how could anyone be jealous of a person who sounded like an electric lawn-mower? I just didn't think that Tammy-Ann took our situation seriously enough, that's all. I wasn't sure that she even believed what we'd told her. And then, when that evening passed without a call and so did the next one, I decided to tell her what I thought of her at school the next day.

'Do not be too hard on her,' Anton said. 'She cannot keep watch all the time. And, who knows? Maybe that Miss Anstruther has not gone out.'

'Don't be a cretin,' I said nastily. 'Tammy-Ann's use-less. I told you that she'd be no help and I was right.'

We'd decided that it would be best if Anton and I spent the next few evenings together in my apartment. As far as Carlos and Flanagan were concerned, we were simply working together on a History assignment, but the real purpose of the arrangement was to save time when Tammy-Ann's call at last came through. I must admit that it was pleasant just being with Anton, even when we were actually working and not just talking or looking into each other's eyes.

We talked a lot during those hours together. He told me more about his life in Venezuela, about the beauty of the country and about his unhappiness at being so far away from his family. And I told him about *my* parents: about the father I barely remembered, and about my mother, who didn't want to see me. Or so it seemed.

'My poor Mel,' Anton whispered then, and gently touched my cheek.

The more I saw of Anton, the more I wondered what I had ever seen in Jordan. Anton was gentle, charming, funny, unpredictable – all the things that Jordan wasn't. Jordan had never made me laugh or made me angry in the way that Anton did. I couldn't remember when I had last enjoyed just *being* with someone. And that's probably why I smiled and said nothing when Anton asked me not to be too hard on Tammy-Ann.

I finally spoke to her about it on Thursday. She'd been avoiding me all day but I managed to catch up with her between English and Art.

'I'm doing my best,' she snapped. 'I can't spend the whole evening staring out of the window, can I?'

I didn't see why not and told her so.

'Oh, grow up, Melanie. It's a stupid idea, anyway. Look, if I see that woman leaving the building, I'll let you know. But I'm not going to spend every minute of my spare time looking out for her. Okay?'

And I had to be content with that. Still, my complaint must have had some effect because that evening, at about nine o'clock, the phone rang in my apartment.

Anton and I exchanged a quick glance and then I ran to answer it before Flanagan could get there.

Tammy-Ann's voice sounded even more piercing on the phone than it did in real life. 'Melanie? The woman's just left the building. She's heading up towards St John's Wood Terrace.'

I tried to keep my voice steady. 'Thanks, Tammy-Ann. I really appreciate your help. I mean it.'

'Think nothing of it, Melanie. Anyway, I did it as a favour to Anton.'

I decided not to lose my temper. Instead I went on, 'You know what to do next, don't you?'

'Sure,' she screeched. 'I'll keep looking out to see if she comes back. If she does, I'll call the Anstruthers' number.'

'That's right. Just let the phone ring twice and then hang up. You've got the number?'

'It was in the book. Anstruther, 12 Park Plaza. Right?'

'Right. And I'll ring you as soon as we get back so you can stop watching.'

'Okay. But make it fast, will you?'

'We'll try. And thanks, Tammy-Ann,' I said again. 'I really mean it.'

She mumbled something and then put down the receiver. I went back to my room and nodded to Anton. 'She's gone out,' I whispered.

He grinned. 'At last. Come on, we must go.'

I turned and headed for the door. And then I stopped short and groaned out loud.

'What's the matter?' Anton asked anxiously.

'It's *Thursday*!' I said. I could have kicked myself for forgetting. Flanagan spent each Thursday evening at a Keep Fit class in a gymnasium somewhere. It was agreed between us that I'd always stay in on Thursday evenings to sit with Theo.

'Can we not leave him?' Anton asked.

'No,' I said quickly. 'I'll have to stay.' And then I remembered something else. 'No, *you'd* better stay.' When Anton started to object, I went on, 'No, you must. That woman might come back and she mustn't find *you*. Don't you see? You'd be walking straight into their hands. You must stay here with Theo.'

'But Melanie, I cannot let you – '

'I'm just going to take a closer look at the apartment door, that's all,' I said. 'And anyway, she's not going to do anything to *me*, is she? *You're* the one she's watching. *You're* the one who's in danger.'

Anton didn't seem convinced. 'I do not like it. It is wrong. This is my problem and – '

'What's that got to do with it?' I said. 'I can manage this as well as you can. Better.'

There was a pause, and then Anton put his arms around me and drew me to him. 'Are you sure?' he whispered. 'Would you really do this for me?'

I nodded, and he smiled. 'All right, then,' he said. 'You go. I will stay with Theo.'

'He's in bed,' I said. 'You shouldn't have any trouble, he sleeps like a log. Anyway, I won't be away long.'

'I will watch from your balcony. And Mel – ' He drew me even closer to him and kissed me gently on the forehead. 'Be careful, please. Promise me you will be careful.'

'Don't worry,' I said huskily, hoping that I sounded more confident than I felt. Then I turned and walked into the hall and let myself out of the flat.

It didn't take me long to walk round to Park Plaza. As I approached the building, I could see Tammy-Ann waiting irritably in the brightly lit lobby. When she saw me, she opened the heavy glass door. We'd agreed that I wouldn't ring her bell as one of her parents might reach the Answerphone before her.

'Where've you been?' she screeched. 'I've been waiting ages.' She peered into the darkness behind me and then asked in a puzzled tone, 'Where's Anton?'

'I had to leave him with Theo,' I said.

Tammy-Ann shrugged, and we walked to the elevator together. 'Good luck,' she said when the lift reached her floor, and I grinned weakly. My heart was thumping in my chest; I felt sure that she would hear it. Then the doors closed again and the elevator sailed slowly upwards to the top floor.

When the doors opened on the top landing, I stayed where I was for a moment and listened. Then I stepped cautiously out of the lift and walked towards the door of apartment twelve. There was no sound at all, not even the mumble of a television set from apartment eleven. Mr and Mrs Rogers were probably asleep, I thought. And their cats as well. When I reached Miss Anstruthers door, I bent down and pressed my ear against it. I had to be sure that there was no one inside. But there wasn't a sound from the apartment. Then I turned my attention to the lock. It was a simple Yale, and I realised then that I'd forgotten to bring a credit card with me. Not that I had one, of course. I knew that Anton didn't have one, either, and I'm sure Flanagan wouldn't have given me one of hers. So it didn't matter anyway. I shrugged, and idly tested the door

101

handle. There was a click, and then, very slowly, the door swung open.

I couldn't believe my eyes. The door wasn't locked. Miss Anstruther had gone out without locking it behind her. I should have stopped then to wonder why she hadn't bothered but I didn't. Instead, I pushed the door further open and peered inside. Ahead of me lay a hallway. There were closed doors on either side but, straight ahead, an open door led into what I assumed was the sitting room. The light was on, and I could see brightly-patterned wallpaper and part of an armchair.

It was now or never. I took a deep breath and stepped into the hall. I stopped for a moment to listen once more but there was no sound at all, apart from my own harsh breathing. Then I closed the front door behind me and walked up the hall towards the sitting room.

The room was empty. It was comfortably furnished but it had a lifeless air about it, as though no one had lived there for a long time. I looked quickly round for clues to the identity of Miss Anstruther but I could find nothing. There were no papers or books or any other signs of human life. Apart from one or two boring pictures of country scenes there weren't even any ornaments. I shivered and crossed to the window. I drew back the curtains and found myself staring at my own block of flats. There, a little below me, was the apartment where I lived. Lights blazed at the sitting room window. The curtains hadn't been drawn and I could see Anton standing there, looking out. I waved to him, and he waved back excitedly and came out on to the balcony. I waved again. I couldn't see his face very clearly but I could just make out the familiar furniture in the room behind him, the pictures and bookshelves and the door to the dining room. And then, with a start, I realised that this was the view that Miss Anstruther would have seen when she looked out of this very window. She would have been watching the penthouse, of course, but she'd be able to see our apartment, too. She had been able to watch every move we made in that room. And then, as I stared at the flat, Theo appeared on the balcony beside Anton, and I frowned. What was he doing there? He shouldn't be up. He ought to be fast asleep, the little tyke. He was talking to Anton now, and pointing to me. I scowled. Why didn't Anton send him back to bed? Just wait till I –

And then the phone rang, and I nearly jumped out of my skin with fright. It rang twice, very loudly, and then stopped.

Oh, my God, I thought. Two rings. She was coming back. Miss Anstruther was coming back. I stepped away from the window and looked desperately round the bare sitting room. What should I do? I must go. I must go at once. I had to get out of that flat. But I might meet her coming out of the lift, or on the stairs. I must hide, then. But where? There was no hiding place at all in that neat, lifeless room. The other rooms, then. The closed doors in the hall.

I ran to the door and into the hallway. I stopped, wondering which door to choose. Ahead of me lay the front door, and I made towards that. I had to get out of the flat. I *had* to –

And then, like a scene in a nightmare, the front door opened. I shut my eyes, hoping against hope that it was all a bad dream and that any minute now I'd wake up in my own room and it would be last Monday and I hadn't finished my essay for Jim Curtis. But when I opened them again, I saw at once that I wasn't dreaming.

Miss Anstruther was standing in the doorway, staring at me, her face pale with shock. Behind her were two men but I didn't pay much attention to them. I couldn't take my eyes off Miss Anstruther.

When at last she spoke, her voice was tight with anger. 'And so we meet again, Miss Melanie Rosidis. I'm sorry but I'm not interested in joining the Cats' Protection League.'

I didn't know what she meant at first and then I remembered our previous encounter. I opened my mouth to say something but, for once, words failed me. What excuse could I possibly give for being in her flat?

'How – how do you know my name?' I said at last.

She laughed harshly then, and walked towards me. The men followed her into the flat and closed the door. I backed away from her into the sitting room. She carried on walking towards me but stopped when I found myself with my back to the window.

'Well?' she said. 'What exactly are you doing here?'

One of the men grinned and said, 'Isn't she – '

'Shut up!' Miss Anstruther barked sharply. 'Leave the talking to me.' Then she gave me an acid smile. 'Come now, Melanie. I'm not going to wait here all night. Why don't you tell me exactly what you're doing here?'

Suddenly I couldn't bear that icy stare a moment longer. I turned in desperation and found that I was facing the window, looking out at our apartment. Anton was still on the balcony, staring back at me. Could he see me? Could he see what was happening? Theo was still beside him, a small figure in striped pyjamas.

There was a sudden gasp behind me, and I turned. Miss Anstruther was staring through the window too, following my gaze. Oh no, I thought. She's seen him. She's seen Anton.

'He's there,' she said curtly. 'We'd better take him now. There's no point in waiting, now that the girl's found us. Go and get him.'

One of the men mumbled something to her and then both of them walked quickly from the room.

I stared at Miss Anstruther in horror and then I screamed, 'No!' I tried to push past her but she was too strong for me. She twisted my arm behind my back until I cried out with pain and then dragged me to the window.

'No, please,' I moaned. 'Don't hurt him. *Please* don't hurt him!'

She said nothing but stared out across the darkness towards the lighted room opposite. Anton had left the balcony now and he and Theo were in the sitting room. What on earth were they doing? Why didn't he come and help me?

'Thanks to you we'll have to do this the messy way,' Miss Anstruther said. 'If you hadn't interfered it would all have been much more civilised.'

I didn't answer but kept my eyes on the room opposite, willing Anton to run. I couldn't see him now; perhaps he was phoning the police. And then he came into view again. He backed into the room, waving his arms excitedly. He was followed by two men, the same two men who had arrived with Miss Anstruther.

'Good, they're inside,' she murmured behind me.

I watched in horror as one of the men hit Anton in the face. The other man disappeared from view for a moment and then came back, dragging Theo behind him. The boy was struggling and shouting, and the man picked him up bodily and carried him from the room. Anton tried to follow them but the second man pulled him back and hit him again. Anton fell, and the man stared down at him for a moment before following the others.

It was like watching a silent movie. A horror movie. I could see everything that happened but I couldn't hear anything. And there was nothing I could do to help. Now the room was empty once more, and Miss Anstruther relaxed her grip slightly. Then I saw Anton again. He had struggled to his feet and staggered onto the balcony. He was staring across at me with eyes wide with horror. And, as he stared, I realised what had happened.

'Oh, my God!' I screamed. 'They've taken Theo! They've taken *Theo*!'

CHAPTER TEN

'They've taken Theo!' I repeated.

I pulled my wrist from Miss Anstruther's grasp and swung round to face her. She seemed surprised by what I'd said.

'Of course,' she said.

'But you're supposed to take Anton,' I said stupidly. 'You were watching *Anton*.'

Miss Anstruther stepped backwards then and gave a harsh laugh. 'Who the hell's Anton?' she asked.

And then everything suddenly fell into place. She hadn't been watching Anton at all. She hadn't been watching the penthouse. She'd been watching *our* flat all the time. Watching us. Watching Theo. Theo had been the intended victim all along, not Anton.

I was to blame. It was all my fault. If I hadn't been so stupid I'd have realised the truth from the start. But it was all Anton's fault, really. He was the one who'd set me on the wrong track with all his stupid talk of kidnappers and bodyguards. He was to blame. I hated him. Hated him.

Miss Anstruther moved towards me once again and I backed away. 'Don't touch me!' I shouted. 'Leave me alone!'

'I don't want to hurt you, Melanie,' she hissed. 'I don't want to hurt you. But I need time to get away. Just a little time. So please, go out onto the balcony.'

I stared at her in horror. 'What are you going to do?'

'There's nothing to worry about.' She pulled open the sliding glass door. 'I just want you to go outside. *Now!*' And she grabbed my arm again and forced it behind my back, and pushed me out through the doorway. Then she slipped back into the sitting room and locked the door behind her.

I was trapped on the balcony. The only way of escape was by jumping to the ground six floors below or by breaking the plate-glass door. Could I manage that without cutting myself? I stared desperately across the gap to our flat. Lights blazed at all the windows but there was no one to be seen. Where was Anton now? What was he doing? I remembered the man hitting Anton and I remembered him falling. Was he all right? Was he badly hurt? Was he – It was stupid of me to blame Anton. I didn't hate him. I loved him. It wasn't his fault at all. It was mine, mine. Oh, please, don't let Anton be hurt . . .

Everything was a bit of a blur after that and I can't remember exactly what happened next. I seem to remember standing at the balcony rail and yelling my head off. And then, after what seemed like hours but probably wasn't, there was movement in the flat behind me and faces appeared at the glass door. There was a sound of breaking glass and then I felt strong arms around me. And I saw Anton's face, his eyes wide with anxiety. There were other faces, too. The young doorman with the fair hair, and Tammy-Ann Ziegler, and other people I didn't recognise. And then I was dimly aware of being hustled through the flat and into the elevator, and of Anton's gentle voice telling me not to worry, and other people milling around me. Then the comfort of the Mercedes, and Carlos peering down at me, looking kind for once. And then another lobby, another elevator, and the familiar calm of our sitting room.

I may have fainted then, I don't know, because the next thing I remember is waking up on the sofa, with Flanagan staring down at me and crying, 'It's all my fault! I should have stayed in!' I tried to tell her that she wasn't to blame but someone else – a doctor, I think – told me to lie back and keep quiet. And always Anton was there, his eyes never leaving my face, his hand in mine.

Then the police came and I had to talk about it. I had to tell them everything. There were two of them, Inspector Someone and another one, a sergeant, who wrote everything down. They weren't wearing uniforms and I remember thinking how suspicious that seemed. Were they really policemen? How could I be sure?

It was then, I think, that the most surprising thing happened. The sitting room door was flung open and a tall red-haired woman dressed in something long and shimmering appeared in the doorway. Behind her was a man in a dinner jacket. It was my mother. I hadn't seen her for days. Trust her to choose that particular moment to make an entrance.

She stared round the room in amazement and then said, 'What's going on? Mel, who *are* all these people?'

And then the noise and crying and questions began again, and I can't remember much after that. My next clear memory is of Anton and I sitting together on the sofa. He was telling me over and over again that I shouldn't blame myself, that it was his fault, his alone.

'But it's not,' I said. 'How were we to know that they wanted Theo and not you? You were the most likely victim. Who would have guessed that they wanted – ² I turned to him in desperation. 'Why Theo? Why did they take Theo? Who on earth would want to take that little boy?'

Anton got up then, I remember, and walked away from me, as if he didn't want me to see his face. He said, 'I think I know who it was. I think I have known for some time.'

Who?' I shouted. 'Why didn't you say something? Why didn't you tell the police?'

He turned to face me, his face taut with pain. 'I have only just realised it,' he said. 'I could not remember – '

I was trembling now. 'What are you talking about? I don't understand!'

Anton led me back to the sofa and we sat down again. He took my hands in his and gazed into my eyes. 'Do you remember when we followed Miss Anstruther to that gallery of famous people? I forget the name – '

I nodded impatiently. 'Yes. Of course I remember.'

'I told you that she met a man there. A man who looked familiar to me.'

'Yes,' I said. 'But you couldn't remember where you'd seen him before.'

'That is right,' he said unhappily. 'I could not remember. Ever since then I have tried to think where I have seen him before. I thought it must be in Venezuela but I am not sure. I could not remember!' He shook his head despairingly. 'It is only tonight that I remember the

110

face. It is tonight, when I am here with Theo in your apartment that I remember at last.'

He stopped then. It was as if he didn't want to tell me who the man was. As if he didn't want me to know.

I grabbed his arm impatiently. 'Well, who was it?'

Anton looked at me sadly. 'It was the man in the photograph in the hall. The man with you on the beach when you were little. It was your father.'

CHAPTER ELEVEN

I didn't go to school the next day, of course. Apart from anything else, none of us wanted to leave the apartment in case news came about Theo while we were out. The police were watching the airports, so they said, and told us that Theo couldn't be smuggled out of the country without their knowledge, but I had my doubts.

I didn't tell anyone about my father at first. I couldn't believe that he would have anything to do with kidnapping his own child. And anyway, how could I betray my own father to the police? But in the end I told Flanagan, because I had to tell *someone*. And she told me not to worry because the police had suspected my father from the first. My mother had told them about the divorce and how angry he had been when my mother was given custody of us both and how he'd tried once before to snatch Theo and take him back to Greece. I hadn't known about that. Flanagan said that I needn't worry about betraying my father because the police were already looking for him. So that was all right, at least.

Abby came to see me after school on Friday. She sidled into my room as though she wasn't sure if I'd be pleased to see her. But I flung my arms around her and we laughed with delight to see each other.

'Tammy-Ann's been telling everyone what happened,'

Abby said. 'She's the centre of attention and, boy, is she loving it.'

'I wanted to tell you, Abby,' I said. 'I wanted to tell you but I promised Anton.'

She nodded and patted my hand. 'So tell me now,' she said. 'Tell me all about it from the beginning. All the gory details.'

And I did. I told her the whole story from beginning to end. I told her all about Anton, of course. I was sure now of my feelings for him, and of his for me. I told her how I had cried in his arms the night before, and how he had held me and comforted me and told me that he loved me.

'I am so sorry, Mel,' he'd said. 'I am sorry about Theo, and about your father – '

'There you go, apologising again,' I sniffed.

Then he kissed me gently and whispered, 'I will never forget how brave you were. I will never forget that you tried to help me.'

'And all the time I should have been helping Theo,' I'd said.

His strong arms encircled me again. 'It is not your fault, Mel. It is not your fault.'

'He's right,' Abby said when I finished telling her. 'It isn't your fault, Mel. You mustn't blame yourself. But I'm glad.' And she patted my hand.

'Glad?'

'About you and Anton.'

I grinned at her like an idiot. 'Yes,' I said. 'It's wonderful.'

It was good to have Abby back in my life again.

After that, Anton arrived, and they were both with me

when Flanagan rushed in to say that Theo was downstairs. Old Cocky Nose had rung through to say that he'd been found wandering in the street outside. To say that Theo was downstairs in the lobby and should he bring him up?

It was on Sunday morning that the phone call came, the call I'd been expecting. He asked me to meet him that afternoon but I didn't know what to say at first. Then at last I said yes and he told me where to go, and I put the receiver down. I called Anton then and asked him to go with me. To be on the safe side.

I found him sitting on a bench halfway up Primrose Hill. It was a cool, sunless afternoon and he looked chilled and miserable.

I sat down beside him and said, 'Hullo, Dad.'

He smiled and said, 'Hi, Midget.' He was the only person who ever called me by that silly childhood nickname. He coughed nervously and went on, 'Thanks for coming. I wanted – I wanted to explain. I want you to understand – to understand why . . .' His voice tailed away into a miserable silence. Then, 'Is Theo okay?' he asked.

I nodded, and he smiled with relief.

'Why did you send him back?' I asked. 'Why did you go to all that trouble and then change your mind?'

My father's eyes suddenly filled with tears. 'I thought it would be different,' he said, so quietly that I could hardly hear him. 'I thought Theo would be pleased to see me. I thought he would be glad to be with me. I didn't realise –' He looked quickly away. 'Theo was scared of me, Midget. He hated me. He was frightened. I couldn't keep a child who hated me, who didn't want to be with me. It was all a mistake. A dreadful mistake.'

114

I didn't say anything. I stared out across the trees towards the zoo and the distant grey haze beyond.

'I should never have done it,' my father said. 'It was wrong, it was cruel, it was – a mistake. I want you to know that.'

'Those people,' I said at last. 'The woman. Who was she?'

He shrugged. 'I don't know. It was all arranged by someone else. I paid them to watch, to pick the right moment to take him. But it was difficult. Theo hardly went out, and never on his own.' He sighed. 'And that woman ruined it all by letting herself be seen. By you. But I'm glad it didn't work out. I'm very glad.'

I stared at him, at the dark-haired stranger who was my father. 'Why didn't you kidnap me?' I asked. 'Why didn't you want *me*?'

He gave a slow, sad smile. 'Theo is my son.'

'So what? I'm your daughter. Didn't you want me?'

My father pulled up his coat collar, and shivered. 'You wouldn't understand. You are too young.'

'I'm sixteen years old,' I said angrily. 'Try me.'

'Theo is my son,' he said softly. 'I need – needed my son. He is my only son.'

'Yes, Theo is your son!' I shouted. 'But I am your daughter. Your only daughter. Why do you want him and not me?'

'You don't understand,' he murmured. 'You don't understand.'

I stood up then and stared down at him. I didn't hate this sad little man. But I didn't love him either. How could I? He was a stranger.

115

I started to walk down the hill but stopped when he called my name.

'Midget, will you come and stay with me this summer? Will you come and visit me in Greece?'

I turned to look at him. 'No,' I said. 'I'm sorry, but I can't. I don't want to. And anyway, I may be going to Venezuela.'

And then I ran down to the bottom of the hill where Anton was waiting.

More Beaver Books

On the following pages you will find some
other exciting Beaver Books to look out for
in your local bookshop

BEAVER BOOKS FOR OLDER READERS

There are loads of exciting books for older readers in Beaver. They are available in bookshops or they can be ordered directly from us. Just complete the form below and send the right amount of money and the books will be sent to you at home.

☐	THE RUNAWAYS	Ruth Thomas	£1.99
☐	COMPANIONS ON THE ROAD	Tanith Lee	£1.99
☐	THE GOOSEBERRY	Joan Lingard	£1.95
☐	IN THE GRIP OF WINTER	Colin Dann	£2.50
☐	THE TEMPEST TWINS Books 1 – 6	John Harvey	£1.99
☐	YOUR FRIEND, REBECCA	Linda Hoy	£1.99
☐	THE TIME OF THE GHOST	Diana Wynne Jones	£1.95
☐	WATER LANE	Tom Aitken	£1.95
☐	ALANNA	Tamora Pierce	£2.50
☐	REDWALL	Brian Jacques	£2.95
☐	BUT JASPER CAME INSTEAD	Christine Nostlinger	£1.95
☐	A BOTTLED CHERRY ANGEL	Jean Ure	£1.99
☐	A HAWK IN SILVER	Mary Gentle	£1.99
☐	WHITE FANG	Jack London	£1.95
☐	FANGS OF THE WEREWOLF	John Halkin	£1.95

If you would like to order books, please send this form, and the money due to:

ARROW BOOKS, BOOKSERVICE BY POST, PO BOX 29, DOUGLAS, ISLE OF MAN, BRITISH ISLES. Please enclose a cheque or postal order made out to Arrow Books Ltd for the amount due including 22p per book for postage and packing both for orders within the UK and for overseas orders.

NAME ....

ADDRESS ....

....

Please print clearly.

Whilst every effort is made to keep prices low it is sometimes necessary to increase cover prices at short notice. Arrow Books reserve the right to show new retail prices on covers which may differ from those previously advertised in the text or elsewhere.

BEAVER BESTSELLERS

You'll find books for everyone to enjoy from Beaver's bestselling range—there are hilarious joke books, gripping reads, wonderful stories, exciting poems and fun activity books. They are available in bookshops or they can be ordered directly from us. Just complete the form below and send the right amount of money and the books will be sent to you at home.

☐	THE ADVENTURES OF KING ROLLO	David McKee	£2.50
☐	MR PINK-WHISTLE STORIES	Enid Blyton	£1.95
☐	FOLK OF THE FARAWAY TREE	Enid Blyton	£1.99
☐	REDWALL	Brian Jacques	£2.95
☐	STRANGERS IN THE HOUSE	Joan Lingard	£1.95
☐	THE RAM OF SWEETRIVER	Colin Dann	£2.50
☐	BAD BOYES	Jim and Duncan Eldridge	£1.95
☐	ANIMAL VERSE	Raymond Wilson	£1.99
☐	A JUMBLE OF JUNGLY JOKES	John Hegarty	£1.50
☐	THE RETURN OF THE ELEPHANT JOKE BOOK	Katie Wales	£1.50
☐	THE REVENGE OF THE BRAIN SHARPENERS	Philip Curtis	£1.50
☐	THE RUNAWAYS	Ruth Thomas	£1.99
☐	EAST OF MIDNIGHT	Tanith Lee	£1.99
☐	THE BARLEY SUGAR GHOST	Hazel Townson	£1.50
☐	CRAZY COOKING	Juliet Bawden	£2.25

If you would like to order books, please send this form, and the money due to:

ARROW BOOKS, BOOKSERVICE BY POST, PO BOX 29, DOUGLAS, ISLE OF MAN, BRITISH ISLES. Please enclose a cheque or postal order made out to Arrow Books Ltd for the amount due including 22p per book for postage and packing both for orders within the UK and for overseas orders.

NAME ....

ADDRESS ....

....

Please print clearly.

Whilst every effort is made to keep prices low it is sometimes necessary to increase cover prices at short notice. Arrow Books reserve the right to show new retail prices on covers which may differ from those previously advertised in the text or elsewhere.